SHORT SHORT STORIES FOR BUSY BUSY PEOPLE

By

Jim McGuirk & Eleanor Leeson

920 7699

Copyright © 2015 Jim McGuirk

ISBN-13: 978-1492309925

ISBN-10: 1492309923

THIS BOOK CONTAINS THEMES AND SUBJECT MATTER THAT IS UNSUITABLE FOR MINORS.

All rights reserved.

The moral right of the authors has been asserted. No part of this publication may be reproduced, stored in a retrieval system, or transmitted in any form or by any means without the prior permission in writing of the authors.

All characters and events in this publication are fictitious and any resemblance to real persons, living or dead, is purely coincidental.

Cover Image Art and Design by Eleanor Leeson.

We would like to thank our son, Jim, and our friend, Jim Moran for their unstinting efforts in proof reading this book.

The Book Is Dedicated To Our Family
Carlene, Denise, Jimmy, Carmen, Leanne, Jamie and Bradley.

We love you more than words can ever say.
XXX

CONTENTS

	Preface	6
1	These Old Stones	8
2	A Day in the Life	13
3	The Woman in Pink	15
4	Granddad's Birthday Party	22
5	Three Kisses for Tom	25
6	If	32
7	How the Dice Fall	34
8	The Dysfunctional Policeman	39
9	Insomnia Drives You Insania	41
10	Valentine	46
11	Young Love	49
12	It Was a Good Year	54
13	The Secret Door	56
14	Goldfinger	61
15	Premonitions	64
16	Seduction	68
17	The Pain	71
18	The Hoodie	76
19	The Journey	80
20	Alone	83
21	In Thought, Word and Deed	87
22	Barricade	90

23	Invisibility	97
24	Tom's Betrayal	100
25	It Sounded Like an Explosion	105
26	Harvest Time	108
27	Spinning Enid	115
28	Bus Stop	120
29	Sermon	125
30	Stag Night	127
31	The Crash	131
32	The Decision	134
33	The Housewife	139
34	The Glowing Embers of Love	142
35	The Inheritance	146
36	Unwelcome Reunion	149
37	The House	155
38	Twins	159
39	A Face in the Crowd	166
40	Cycle	169
41	The Party	173
42	What Happened in the Playground	177
43	The Prisoner's Tale	181
44	Ted Watkins, the Salt of the Earth	187

PREFACE

The title for this book came to me as I settled in my seat for a bus journey home. I had a small book of science fiction stories in my pocket and decided to read one. I guessed the trip would take about half an hour, so I opened the book on the contents page and counted between the page numbers to see which were the shortest stories. If I gauged it right I could perhaps find one I could just finish before my stop.

This was nothing new to me. Even as a young boy opening my newest *Pan Book of Horrors*, I would check the contents page, work out which was the shortest of the short stories, then work my way up, story by story, to the longest.

Whether I had a short span of attention or required instant gratification, I do not know. What I do know is that many readers share this habit. Most people I have discussed the idea with seem to do the same thing, so we can't *all* be wrong ... can we?

With the above in mind, I thought it would be a good idea to produce a book which contained only the shortest of short stories. These are ideal for people to read when they have a small amount of time to fill and want something to occupy their minds.

The result is this collection of widely varying stories which I am sure will provoke further thought and stimulate the mind. Most of the stories can be read in fifteen to twenty minutes - some as little as five or ten, so it could be the perfect book to have in your hand-luggage or briefcase as those unexpected delays jump out and ambush you just when you need them least.

Thanks for buying this book and we hope it gives you a lot of enjoyment.

Kind regards,
Jim McGuirk and Eleanor Leeson.

THESE OLD STONES

Grace's aging knees were giving her the usual twinges as she knelt on the worn padded hassock of her village church. Once the Sunday Morning prayers were over, the vicar invited the small congregation to sit as he prepared to deliver his sermon.

Simon, Grace's twelve-year-old grandson, immediately stood and took his grandmother's elbow as she eased herself up onto the polished wooden bench behind her.

"Are you comfy Nan?" he whispered.

She turned to him and smiled.

"Yes I'm fine thank you Son."

Satisfied that his Nan was comfortable, Simon sat down, folded his arms and awaited the vicar's spiritual guidance.

Grace had looked after Simon since he was two years old. His mum, Tracy, and his dad, Mike, were both killed when the driver of an articulated lorry had fallen asleep at the wheel and ploughed into them. To make matters worse, Grace lost her husband, George, to illness the following year.

It had been the worst time of her life and she seriously doubted her desire and ability to carry on living. She knew the grief would never leave her but she hoped that as time went on she would learn to cope with it, if only for Simon's sake.

The only comfort she had from the emotional wreckage was watching Simon grow into the fine, considerate boy he had become today. She often thought how proud her daughter Tracy, and son-in-law Mike, would be if they could see him now.

She looked slowly around the three hundred year old church, savouring the beauty of its magnificent architecture. She thought about all the people who had used the church in hope and in thanksgiving. She thought about all the christenings, marriages and funerals. The overwhelming desire to connect in some way with departed loved ones. She thought about her own hopes and her own strong belief of a joyous reunification in a life yet to come.

These old stones have seen it all, she thought, *they've seen our sad times and they've seen our happy times.*

It seemed to her that she knew all the vicar's sermons by heart, so she passed the time by looking around at the church and the congregation. Glancing down at Simon, she noticed that his cheeks looked a bit flushed. She followed the direction of his gaze and saw that his classmate, Susan Lynch, was smiling at him.

Grace gasped in surprise. *Of all the children in the village,* she thought, *why did it have to be Susan Lynch?*

She had never told anybody about her teenage romance with Susan's Grandfather, Ted Lynch, and how he had broken her heart. She remembered her mother telling her that he was no good and she wasn't to see him again

Grace, of course, thought she knew better and used to sneak out to meet him while telling her mother she was going to a friend's house. Ted had told her that they would marry one day, and Grace, in her youthful naivety, had believed him. When Ted suddenly left the village without telling anybody Grace was heartbroken. The fact that he didn't even say goodbye crushed her emotionally. It was a long time before she learned to trust anybody romantically again.

Rumours of Ted's exploits drifted back to the village from time to time and he never seemed to be out of trouble, but she clung on to every scrap of news about him, hoping that one day he would return. Two years later Ted did return to the village, bringing with him a wife and a baby son, but by this time Grace had met George, the real love of her life. George showed Grace that true love was about giving, not taking as Ted was prone to do.

As she immersed herself deeply in her youthful memories, Grace once again felt the lightness and vitality of those early days. Then suddenly, from out of nowhere, George's voice was echoing around inside her head.

"You're right love," she heard him say, "these old stones *have* seen it all."

"I love you George," she said out loud, "I love you so much."

She noticed Simon's puzzled expression as he looked into her face.

Here I go again, she thought snapping herself out of it. *They'll be carting me off soon.*

Making their way home from the church, Grace could contain herself no longer.

"I see Susan Lynch was in church again this week."

Simon was hesitant. "Err, yes Nan."

"She's a nice girl isn't she?" Grace went on.

Simon didn't answer, but Grace knew from his bright red cheeks that he was smitten.

She frowned. *I hope she's a nicer person than her Grandfather was*, she thought.

As the years rolled by, Simon's development into adulthood was contrasted by Grace's advancing old age, but she never wanted for anything. Simon and Susan were always there for her, bringing light and happiness into her remaining years. Grace eventually grew to love Susan for her kind and caring ways, and when she and Simon announced their engagement at Susan's twenty-first birthday party, Grace was overjoyed.

Three months after the engagement, the years took their ultimate toll and Grace passed away peacefully in her sleep. Simon was distraught. It took all the strength and support that Susan could muster to help him over his grievous loss, but eventually, she eased his pain and they started looking forward to their wedding once again.

After that, the months seemed to race by as they immersed themselves in what seemed to be a never ending list of preparations. Susan's brother, Tom, who had come to regard Simon also as a brother, was both delighted and honoured to be asked to take on the role of best man and agreed instantly.

Soon there was nothing else to be done. Their day had arrived.

As Simon and Tom stood nervously at the altar awaiting the arrival of the bride, Simon turned to Tom and spoke,

"I wish Nan could have been here," he said.

The church organ burst into life as the powerful strains of Richard Wagner's Bridal Chorus filled the village church. Simon turned and looked behind him. Beaming with love and pride, he saw Susan on her father's arm, slowly approaching the altar in time to the music.

She's beautiful, he thought, *I love her so much.*

Still smiling uncontrollably, he turned back to face the altar.

"Yes," he said aloud, "these old stones have seen it all."

He paused.

What a strange thing to say, he reflected, *I wonder why I said that?*

This story was co-written by Mrs Pat Johnson, a friend and fellow member of our writing group at the Netherton Activity Centre.

A DAY IN THE LIFE

'I'm staying out of her way today. I couldn't stand another day like yesterday; she's becoming obsessed. A few months ago it was D. I. Y. day in, day out. That was followed by the keep fit craze. We were walking and jogging ten miles every day. I wondered if she was just tiring me out so I wouldn't bother her at bedtime. Now this obsession with her pet snake.
Don't get me wrong, I really love her and I've put up with her little obsessions ever since she turned up. I put it down to a mild form of OCD, but this latest one's gone well over the top. I've had enough today so I've found myself a good hiding place. She won't find me here; she never comes near the vegetable patch. Too much like hard work!
To be honest I don't know why I bother growing vegetables, she's never learned to cook and she just boils everything to a pulp. These spuds look nice though; I might bake a couple of them for our dinner.'
He picks two large, smooth potatoes and wipes off the loose soil. Standing up, he puts them in the pocket of his gardening jacket.
Stretching out his arms, he yawns in relaxed contentment, savouring the gentle warming rays of the early morning sunshine.
He winces as she calls out at the top of her parrot-like voice.

"Darling! Yoo-hoo! Darling, where are you. I can't find you."

He darts behind the runner bean frames, squats down and hunches his head and shoulders out of sight. Holding his breath, he watches as she walks along the main path looking left and right as she passes the smaller walkways that lead into the raised vegetable beds.

She walks past without seeing him.

"Phew, that was close," he says in a loud, relieved whisper.

He stands up slowly, grateful that the lush crop of runner beans provided him with such an excellent hiding place and makes his way back to the house. Once there, he washes the potatoes in the kitchen sink. His peace is short lived.

"There you are!" she squawks, "I've been looking everywhere for you."

"I've been down in the vegetable patch," he answers with a cringe.

"Well, never mind that now ... I've picked one."

"You've what?"

"I've picked one of those apples, it's lovely, have a taste."

"No, we're not supposed to."

"Go on, just one bite. It won't do any harm."

"Oh, go on then, just one bite. I suppose it'll be OK. Hmm, I have to say, Eve, it's the nicest apple I've ever tasted."

THE WOMAN IN PINK

The Tank landed a perfect left uppercut on his opponent's jaw and watched his lights go out as he slumped heavily to the canvas.
Old Henry Cooper himself would have been proud of that one, he thought as the referee began his superfluous count.
As soon as the fight was over, the medical team clambered into the ring, and with some urgency, tended to the ex-world bantamweight champion. He eventually regained consciousness but was taken to hospital as a precaution.
The Tank, alias Walter Simpkins, strutted around the ring like an arrogant peacock drinking in the adulation of the fevered crowd.
Walter knew that the next few days would be a blur of activity. The press, the television people, and the whole world would want a slice of him - after all, it wasn't every day a new world champion was crowned. This was the part he didn't like. It was one thing to win the fight and show off for a bit in front of his fans, but the intrusion into his private life didn't sit well with him at all. Once the fight was over, he liked to go home and close his front door on the world.
He thought back to the first time he put on a pair of boxing gloves. He was nine years old and the idea of standing toe to toe with another boy, trading

punches, terrified him. He was being bullied at school on a regular basis and although he tried to keep it from his parents, it was difficult to hide black eyes and swollen lips.

His father's desperation led them to visiting the local boxing club. Once he learned to trust the club coach and overcome his initial fears, it became clear to everybody who watched him train that he had an abundance of natural talent. The school bullying stopped almost overnight and he became much more assertive.

Now, here he was, twelve years later, the bantamweight champion of the world. He wished with all his heart that his mother and father could have shared in his success. He knew they would have been so proud.

He left the boxing arena by one of the side doors, hoping to slip away unnoticed but when he saw the media circus surrounding his car, he knew it wasn't going to happen. He went back inside and rang a taxi. Fifteen minutes later, wearing a baseball cap and dark glasses, he grinned as he passed the paparazzi. They could watch his car all night if they wanted - he would pick it up the following morning.

After nearly an hour of listening to the taxi driver rhapsodising about the fight, and how good the new 'champ' was, they turned into Walter's driveway.

Once inside his home, Walter had a few stiff drinks - his reward for all the pre-fight training and abstinence - and went to bed.

The following morning, Walter lay awake hardly daring to believe that he had won his championship fight the previous night. He felt his face for swellings and sore spots where he may have been hit. There were none.

He felt a sudden surge of pride that he had protected himself so well. He had won a world title without his opponent laying a telling glove on his face. He quivered with excitement. It was time to relax and enjoy himself in the best way he knew how.

Outside the gates at the end of his driveway, the world's reporters were gathered; all hoping for a different angle to their story. It wasn't enough that The Tank had become world champion. The reporters wanted more. They wanted to rip his private life apart and lay it bare for all the world to see.

They surged forward as the electronic gates opened and a pink mini drove out from the driveway and on to the main road.

Cameras flashed almost in unison as they tried to photograph the beautiful, blond haired woman who was driving.

"Who the hell is that?" asked Jeremy Jinnet, the new Daily Stun newspaper reporter.

"That's his sister," replied Simon Stable of The Guardian Gazette. "We've been trying to get close to her for years, to find out what makes him tick, but she won't even honour us with a 'No comment'."

"She's gorgeous," Jeremy went on.

"I know," Simon continued, "the strange thing is, since he won last night's fight and became champion, the whole world's media has been on his tail and nobody can find out anything about her. We're beginning to think his parents might have adopted her shortly before they passed away."

"I'll crack her," Jeremy boasted.

"Do you really think so?" Simon scoffed.

"I do," Jeremy went on, "for one, she doesn't know I'm a reporter, and two," he stood back and posed with his hands on his hips, "how could she resist this?"

Simon laughed aloud but Jeremy was serious.

Jeremy practically camped outside The Tank's house for the next few days, waiting for an opportunity to speak to the boxer's sister. He watched the champ come and go many times, but never his sister. Then, on the third day at 9pm, the gates opened and the pink mini emerged.

Jeremy followed at a safe distance to avoid being noticed. He stayed with the mini until it stopped outside the Pink Pelican nightclub and watched as the attractive blond locked her car then made her way into the club. She was even more beautiful than he remembered.

I'm going to have some fun with this one, he thought, *and a world exclusive into the bargain.*

He followed her inside and waited for the opportunity to introduce himself. He watched as she bought herself a drink, sat on a bar stool, and took a

sip.
When she was settled, he approached her.
"Hi," he said, "I'm Jeremy, can I get you another?"
"No thanks," she said, "I'm driving."
Jeremy ordered himself a drink and struck up a conversation. They spent the next few hours chatting and getting to know each other. He was so taken; he almost forgot why he was there - to get an exclusive on the new world champion.
After a while, he casually steered the conversation in that direction.
"Did you see the fight the other night?"
"Yes"
"The Tank was brilliant wasn't he?"
"I suppose so."
"No 'suppose so' about it, he was brilliant," Jeremy asserted.
"You seem impressed by The Tank. Would you like to meet him?" she said.
"I'd love to." Jeremy said, getting excited.
"Come home with me," she said turning away, "I'll take you to meet him."
Jeremy gazed at her and followed behind, mesmerised by her perfect legs and pink mini skirt.
She seems to have a thing for pink, he thought.
He decided not to mention his own car and resolved to collect it the following day. She opened the passenger door for him and he strapped himself in. She got in the driver's side and they drove off. There was a lull in the conversation but Jeremy hardly

noticed.

He couldn't believe his luck. Not only was he going the get a lucrative scoop on The Tank, but he might get the chance to spend the night with his gorgeous sister too.

They drove through the gateway and up to The Tank's house. He followed her in and she poured a couple of drinks.

"Where's The Tank," he asked.

"Later," she said, "before that, you and me have got some unfinished business."

She took hold of his tie and led him playfully upstairs. Her room was dominated by a king sized four-poster bed. She undressed him, pushed him onto the bed and used his necktie to tie his right wrist to one of the posts on the bed. She lifted her short skirt and unhooked one of her stockings from her suspender belt then used the stocking to tie his other wrist to the opposite bedpost.

Lying there naked, Jeremy's proud physical display made it plain how excited he was, he could not have hidden it even if he wanted to. He watched as she continued to undress in front of him.

He first started to feel a bit uneasy when she took off her bra and her boobs disappeared. His unease escalated to abject fear when she took off her knickers and he saw that her excitement matched his, inch for inch, and manifested itself in the very same way.

She pulled off her blond wig to reveal a head of closely cropped thick, black hair.

"Meet The Tank Jeremy," she said, her voice now an octave lower, "now let's have some fun."

GRANDAD'S BIRTHDAY PARTY

I went to my granddad's hundred and fourth birthday party last week. At sixty-three years of age you might think I'm too old to be going to birthday parties, but the fact is, mum and dad went too. Mum's eighty-three and dad's eighty-four. Granddad had three sons and three daughters so we've branched out into quite a large family. I have two uncles and three aunts. Mum and dad had six children, three girls and three boys, so I have two brothers and three sisters. I have six children of my own and forty-two nieces and nephews. With all *their* children and the great, great grandchildren, all the wives, partners and significant others, there were two-hundred-and-eighty-two people attending the party. Each of them were prepared to set aside the time and make the effort to come and celebrate granddad's birthday. How good is that?

We booked Bootle town hall for the occasion as no other venue was big enough to stage it and handle that number of guests. What a day it turned out to be! We started at one o'clock with a sit down silver service meal. During the meal, various family members and friends stood up and gave speeches, all of which told tales relating to different parts of granddad's life.

Most of the stories were true, or so I've been told, but one of the most remarkable was the fact that our family, the Huntingdon-Smythes, had almost become extinct with granddad being the last of the line, but granddad and grandma Matilda had other ideas - hence the large turnout to his birthday party. By five o'clock, we had all eaten our fill and finished off over three hundred bottles of wine. After this, we moved into the main hall. There was a slight lull in the proceedings as everybody started to chill out a bit. Some of the younger family members were introducing themselves to each other as they had never met before, while others were re-establishing contact with those they had not seen for a long time. A constant stream of camera flashes lit up the large hall as dozens of would be photographers were walking around snapping new family memories for years yet to come. Some guests went home to freshen up, only to return later for the evening and nighttime sessions. The constant chatter was so loud that it drowned out the background music completely.

Time soon passed, and before we knew it afternoon had drifted smoothly into late evening. The lights were dimmed and the disco started blasting out heavy beat music. It was impossible not to dance! Before long there was a seething mass of humanity boiling away, not only on the small dance floor next to the stage, but also in the spaces between the tables and chairs, anywhere in fact, where there was a flat, unoccupied space.

Then, when everyone had had their fill of the Macarena, The Birdie Song and the disc jockey's silly backward baseball cap, it was time for the buffet. The covering cloths came off to loud gasps of appreciation and applause as the long line of tables tempted us with such culinary delights as would not be out of place in a Dickens novel. The DJ played some easy listening background music as we stuffed our faces for the second time that day. Next came a karaoke session. With tonsils well lubricated and inhibitions beaten to a pulp by alcohol, the usual procession of Frank Sinatras, Dean Martins, Elvises, Chers, Madonnas and the rest, rendered confident, if slightly slurred performances.

The last hour or so was taken up with ever popular sixties music which always seems to cut across the age barrier. Eventually, the day took its toll; the dancing slowed and ground to a halt. The drinking stopped - apart from the diehards who had doubled up on last orders. It was now time to wind down the celebrations and head for home. Outside the Town Hall as the crowd jostled, said goodnight, lit up that clamoured for cigarette and waited for their taxis, all were agreed what a great success Granddad's birthday party had been.

Granddad himself couldn't attend of course. Unfortunately, he caught pneumonia and died when he was thirty-five.

THREE KISSES FOR TOM

"Morning Bob," said Vera Riley in her ever-friendly way, "how's Trixie today?"

"Not so bad thanks, Vera. The vet thinks she should be back to normal in a few days. She always was too nosy for her own good. Falling down that well could have been the end of her if it weren't for young Tom from the orphanage."

"Yes," replied Vera, "cheeky young fellow he might well be, but he certainly did a good deed that day, even if he shouldn't have been there himself."

"Yes, well I for one am glad he skipped school that day, or my old Trixie could have been stuck down that well for days. It doesn't bear thinking about. My evenings would be very lonely after I've closed up shop if it wasn't for her. She's my only company since my daughter Louise left home and I lost the missus, God rest her soul. Anyway Vera, what can I get you?"

"Just a quarter of Spam and a small brown loaf please Bob," replied Vera, "Oh! And a quarter of hard-boiled sweets, might as well treat myself."

Bob placed the groceries in a plastic bag and handed them to her.

"Bye then Bob, give Trixie a big pat from me."

Outside the wind was getting colder and Vera pulled up her collar.

As she was leaving the shop, Stan from the Ironmongers entered, with a face like thunder.

"Has that scallywag, Tom Schofield, been in here Bob?" he asked.

"No," replied Bob, "why?"

"He's just been in my place, took a box of fire-lighters, and ran off without paying for them. If you see him, hold on to him and give me a shout will you. That lad's gonna end up in trouble one of these days, you mark my words," he called out as he headed back to his own shop.

Wonder why he stole fire-lighters? Bob pondered, *what use are they to him? Living in a kid's home, he can't have much use for something like that. Unless ... No!*

Bob pulled himself back to reality.

He wouldn't do anything that stupid surely. He's naughty sometimes, but he's not a wicked lad.

For the rest of the morning Bob's thoughts constantly drifted back to Tom, wondering just what a young lad would want with fire-lighters. By one O'clock, he could stand it no longer, and, although it was unusual for him to close at lunchtime, today he'd had enough.

He closed up shop and set off to see what he could find out for himself. He checked on Trixie then made his way down to the children's home. Gingerly, he knocked on the huge, uninviting front door - not quite knowing what excuse he was going to give for asking Tom's whereabouts without getting him into trouble.

"Hello, can I help you?" a voice called from behind the door.

"Errm ...Yes, I'm looking for Tom ... Tom Schofield."
A small white-faced girl put her head around the door.
"Tom's not here, everyone's been looking for him."
"OK Thanks," Bob said, "sorry to be any trouble ... bye."
Bob didn't feel like going back to his shop. Even though it was bitterly cold, he decided to go for a walk along the riverside. Half-way along the river path, Bob was suddenly startled by the sound of a front door being slammed shut. He looked up and saw Tom coming down old Ma Thomson's path. He was heading back towards the children's home. Bob stood back, not knowing whether to call after him, or to call on old Ma Thomson to check if everything was OK. He found himself knocking on Ma Thomson's door.
The old woman lived alone and very rarely ventured out. She had a relative would call to pick up her shopping and do a few chores once or twice a week.
"Hello!" Bob shouted, "Is anybody there? Mrs Thomson, are you there? It's Bob from the village shop."
"Lift the latch and come on in," answered a feeble voice.
Please let her be alright, thought Bob as he followed her instructions to enter the house.
"Hello Bob, it's been some time since I've seen you. Sit down and pour yourself a cuppa. Young Tom's just made me a fresh pot."

"Tom? ... Tom Schofield you mean?" said Bob in a surprised voice.

"Yes, why, is something wrong? He's alright isn't he?" asked Mrs Thomson.

"Sure, he's fine; I just wondered what he was doing here."

"Well," replied Ma, "he comes here quite often. I sometimes wonder how I'd manage without him. Take today for instance, I couldn't get the fire going. I'd run out of fire-lighters - and money. Tom offered to get some for me. I'd be sitting here freezing if it weren't for him. He's such a good lad. It's a shame he's in that kid's home instead of being with a family who would appreciate just what a fine boy he is. Anyway Bob, was there a reason why you called today, or were you just passing?"

"Just passing Ma, just passing."

Bob felt too ashamed to tell her the real reason for knocking at her door. That he thought Tom had caused her some harm or stolen something from her, when, in reality, he had no reason to think such a thing. To the best of his knowledge, Tom had never done him or anybody else any harm, in fact, the opposite was true. He had saved Trixie's life. The only thing left in his life that Bob loved.

He finished his tea with Ma Thomson then said good-bye and left. He still felt so ashamed for thinking such nasty things about Tom.

Before he returned to his own shop, he called in to see Stan at the Ironmongers.

"Stan," he said, "there's been a misunderstanding over the fire-lighters. Here's the money for them. Tom was getting them for Ma Thomson. Is that OK now?"

"Well, I don't know," said Stan, "it doesn't alter the fact that he stole them."

"Let's just let it go, Stan. Just this once ... Just for me." Bob pleaded.

"OK Bob," replied Stan, "but you're too soft by far."

Bob returned to his own shop but never re-opened that afternoon. Instead, he sat with Trixie on his lap and stroked her head, grateful he still had her. He was still feeling ashamed of the things he had thought young Tom capable. He decided he had to see him to thank him properly for saving Trixie, something he hadn't got round to doing.

How could I have been so thoughtless? he asked himself.

The next morning Bob returned to the children's home. This time he was taken into the Matron's room. It was such a large place and seemed so quiet considering it was a children's home. The Matron, a slightly built woman, came into her office and introduced herself to Bob. He returned the courtesy.

"What can I do for you?" she asked.

"I'd like to speak to Tom Schofield," he replied, "he saved my dog, Trixie, last week and I never thanked him properly."

"I'm sorry," replied the Matron, "you can't see Tom right now. I'm afraid his privileges have been withdrawn for a week because of his misbehaviour.

He went missing yesterday without permission and refuses to tell us where he's been."

"Oh!" said Bob, "if I were to tell you where he'd been, could I speak to him then?"

"Well that depends," replied Matron.

Bob decided to tell her anyway. All about the good deeds Tom had been doing for Ma Thomson. It somehow slipped his mind to mention how Tom had got the fire-lighters.

"Well this does put a different light on things," said Matron. "I'll get someone to fetch Tom for you."

"Matron!" called Bob, "just before you leave, could you tell me how Tom came to be here? What happened to his family?"

"That we don't know," she replied. "Schofield's not his real name, it's one *we* gave him. His mother abandoned him when he was only tiny. There was a note attached to his clothing that simply said,

'Take good care of him, I have to go away.'

It was signed with three kisses."

Bob gulped. "Good Lord!" he sighed, "could I see the note? Do you still have it?"

"Why yes," replied Matron, "we have everything Tom had on him when we found him."

She left the room and returned with a small bundle of clothes in a shabby cardboard box and a note written on blue note-paper. It had been torn from a wire bound notepad and had a jagged edge along the top. Bob's face went pale and a tear rolled down his cheek.

"Are you all right?" asked Matron. "Do you want a glass of water?"

As Bob looked up, he put his hand into his left breast pocket and pulled out his wallet.

Then he took out a neatly folded, well-worn, piece of blue note-paper from the same pad and handed it to the matron. She carefully unfolded it and read the words aloud. It simply read,

'Dear Mum and Dad, take good care of yourselves. I have to go away. Love, Louise.'

It was signed with three kisses.

IF

Roggie entered the packed canteen, lumbered over to the table where his co-pilot, Negs, was sitting and joined him. "Thanks for getting the meals in Negs." He grunted. Pale green saliva flowed freely from his open mouth and down onto his jagged reptilian scales as he surveyed the huge plate of ape meat which lay before him.

"A bit scary up there today wasn't it?" he said as he tore apart the putrefied flesh on his plate and placed a piece into his mouth.

"I'll say," replied Negs, "it's a good job we had the nuclear explosives on board. Non-nuclear wouldn't have deflected it enough." Roggie took a long look around the canteen. "There are about two hundred people in here, and not one of them realises how close we came to extinction today! You and I, Negs, are the true unsung heroes of your childhood science fiction comics!"

Roggie and Negs were two of the response pilots for the Astronomical Surveillance Laboratory. It was their job to intercept meteorites that were on a collision path with Earth. Normally their task was routine. It was just a matter of exploding a small charge on the surface of any threatening space debris and changing its direction enough for it to miss their home planet, but today had unnerved both them and their Earthbound colleagues at the ASL.

They had used all of their firepower and had only just managed to deflect today's target – a large asteroid flung out of orbit from a close encounter with Jupiter.

As Roggie and Negs wound down with a savoury cup of half-congealed ape blood, Negs noticed that Roggie was deep in thought. "What's troubling you?" he said.

"Nothing's troubling me really," replied Roggie. "It's just something one of the boffins at the ASL said when we were being debriefed. He said that 65 million years ago there was a huge meteorite on a collision course with Earth, and just by chance, a glancing blow from a small comet changed its direction enough to prevent a direct hit."

"That must happen all the time," Negs replied, "there's nothing unusual about that!"

"It's not just that," Roggie went on, "it's what he said afterwards. He said that they'd run a computer simulation and if that particular meteorite had hit, then only a small amount of reptilian life would have survived due to the sun being blocked out with high levels of atmospheric dust. The computer model also suggested that conditions would have been more favourable for apes, like the one you've just had for your dinner, and that they might even have evolved far enough to become the most intelligent beings on Earth."

Their long thin reptilian tongues uncurled as they both hissed with laughter.

HOW THE DICE FALL

Matilda picked a corner table with a good view of the door so that she could see who was coming and going. She wondered if she'd recognise him after forty-three years.

Fifty minutes later, she looked at her watch and scowled. She was half way through a second pot of tea when she decided to leave. It was then he arrived. She watched him scanning the large cafe until his eyes settled on her. She could tell he was shocked when he saw her. She was sixty-nine years old now, and looked every year of it.

"Hi Mat," he said. "Sorry I'm late, but It's hell out there, the traffic's backed up all along the freeway."

His broad American accent took her by surprise, but the fact that he called her Mat annoyed her intensely. She tried not to show it. She had never liked the name Matilda, but it was infinitely better than Mat.

"Then why did you pick this place to meet? Haven't you ever noticed that roadside cafes have lots of passing traffic? That's how they make their money. Anyway, you were always late."

He took off his coat, sat down at her table and reached across clasping her hands. She pulled away sharply. He fought hard not to react.

"I see you already have a drink," he said, "do you want anything to go with it, a sandwich or a piece of cake perhaps?"

"Look Tony, don't try and turn this into a social occasion," she replied brusquely. "Just tell me why you wanted to meet me here?"

"I'm sorry," he said, "I didn't mean to upset you, I'll just get myself a coffee."

His spirits dampened, he made his way to the counter and ordered. He stood wondering how to approach her. Last night he had it all so clear in his mind, but there was something about reality that always messed up your plans. He paid for his coffee and made his way back to the table deep in thought.

"I came to apologise," he said.

He saw her eyes start to fill up. There was a long pause then she responded.

"You came all the way from America to apologise? It's a bit late for that isn't it? You should have apologised forty-three years ago."

"I was just a kid," he replied defending himself, "a seventeen year old kid."

"You were a Kid when it suited you, a kid who couldn't be trusted to keep his mouth shut. Anyway, as I said, it's a bit late now. Is your conscience weighing you down or something?" she said spitefully.

He took a deep breath and started to explain.

"I've never had the chance before," he said. "By the time you came out of prison my parents had emigrated to the States and forced me to go with them. Their position at the hospital became untenable once the tabloids got hold of it."

"Untenable! There's a nice word, don't you mean we embarrassed the shit out of them?" she interrupted. "How did you find me?"
"I hired a private detective."
"A private detective? That must have cost you; you must have a good job to be able to afford a private detective."
"I'm an English teacher, the same as you were."
They both sat in silence for a few seconds before she spoke again.
"How ironic," she said, glaring at him. "The same as I was before you ruined my life you mean," she continued.
"Hang on," he protested, "there *were* two of us you know, and you were twenty-six years old at the time."
"I was in love," she said showing her gentler side, "if I hadn't been your teacher nobody would have batted an eyelid. You were seventeen, nearly eighteen in fact, and I was twenty-six. All perfectly legal for most people, but because I was your teacher, it's suddenly seen as the crime of the century. You were old enough join the army and fight for your country, but heaven forbid you have an intimate relationship with your teacher."
She broke down as a flood of tears flowed unhindered down her cheeks. He reached across the table and clasped her hands again. This time she didn't pull away.
"Why did you have to blurt it all out?" she said

through her sobs. "All you had to do was to stay quiet and after a while we would have been free to show our true feelings."

"As I said, I came to apologise. It's not my fault people create stupid laws that make no sense."

"No," she said dabbing her cheeks, "but if you'd returned the loyalty I had for you, we'd have been happy. We may well have still been together."

He hung his head in silence acknowledging his guilt and she knew it was time to strike.

"Did you ever marry, Tony?" she said softly.

He nodded affirmatively.

"Yes, it didn't last though. She couldn't have kids and took it out on me. She didn't stop to think that I might have wanted them too. We tried fostering but it didn't work out and she left me."

Her mind was now working overtime.

"We have a daughter you know."

"What?" he gasped.

"I had her in prison. Her name's Susan, she's beautiful. She's the spitting image of you."

"Oh my Lord!" he exclaimed, "when can I see her?"

"You'll have to ask *her*, she's forty-two now you know. We also share four grandchildren, two boys and two girls."

"Where are they, where do they live?" he asked eagerly.

"Unfortunately," she replied, "I don't know. When she was old enough to understand what I'd done with my life she just upped and left. She was so ashamed of me; she didn't even invite me to her wedding.

I had to satisfy myself with the snippets of news I heard from mutual acquaintances. I've never seen our grandchildren."

"Where are they now?" he asked.

"I've no idea. Ten years ago, I tried to get to see them and when I threatened legal action the whole family seemed to disappear off the face of the Earth."

"Didn't you try to find out where they'd gone?" he said, showing his disappointment.

"No," she said sharply, "by that time the message had finally sunk in. I was fifty-nine at the time and decided it would be a waste of the rest of my life."

There was an awkward silence and she spoke again.

"Perhaps you could get that private detective of yours to find them - he seems to know his job."

"Perhaps he can," he said, quickly standing up, "this changes everything, I'll get onto it right away. What are our grandchildren's names?"

Her eyes glinted as she replied.

"She married a man called John Smith, so all the surnames are Smith. There's Peter, the eldest, then it's Susan, John and Mary."

He apologised again, said a hurried goodbye and rushed out of the cafe.

An evil grin spread across Matilda's face. She knew Tony would spend the rest of his life searching for his non-existent daughter and grandchildren.

THE DYSFUNCTIONAL POLICEMAN

Detective Inspector Guy Prince scowled as he walked down the steps of Poolchester Crown Court. He had just wasted yet another day of his life giving evidence in the ongoing farce known as British Justice. He stepped onto the pavement and slowly turned to look in disgust at the pompous, sandstone eunuch of a building which once housed a judiciary that had the power to hand down death penalties, adequate prison sentences, and, if deemed appropriate, the cat of nine tails and the birch. All useful and effective tools employed in the ongoing battle to protect the public from the amoral predators of society. Not any more though, the building was a hollow sham of its former days. The modern day vociferous do-gooders had rendered it useless.

Guy stiffened in anger as Bart Callow came through the revolving doors followed by his unsavoury friends. They were laughing and joking loudly among themselves.

Callow's eyes locked onto Guy's.

"Coming for a celebratory drink Princey," Callow shouted sarcastically.

Guy thought back to the crime which had led to this failed prosecution. He remembered visiting the victim, eighty-nine year old Ethel Malone, shortly after she came out of intensive care. She had lost an eye, been raped, and then beaten to a bruised pulp by a drug crazed Bart Callow.

This, however, seemed less important to her than the fact he had stolen her wedding ring. Her last link with her deceased husband. It was this wedding ring on which the case hinged. Guy found it in a pawnbroker's shop. The pawnbroker had identified Callow as the seller and agreed to give evidence, but following a visit from Callow's cronies, he suddenly clammed up, hence the collapse of the prosecution's case.

Two days later, Detective Inspector Prince and Detective Sergeant Jones surveyed the aftermath of a brutal murder as they waited for the arrival of the Scene of Crime Officers.

Detective Sergeant Jones couldn't understand why Guy Prince was being so reckless when it came to the preservation of the scene of the crime.

Guy Prince knew that in the normal scheme of things, his off-duty behaviour the previous evening had been most unbefitting for a serving police officer. It was contrary to everything he had learned and been taught since his days as a cadet. He was now a dysfunctional policeman. He also knew that this particular dysfunctional policeman had made the world a better place – a much better place.

Detective Sergeant Jones stared into the grey face of the victim.

"Bart Callow," he mused aloud, "that name rings a bell ... I wonder who he upset?"

Guy slowly turned away in an effort to hide his grin.

INSOMNIA DRIVES YOU INSANIA

Sebastian turned over, switched on the light and picked up his book from the bedside cabinet. He rearranged his pillows, moved into a sitting position and opened his thick, dog-eared paperback copy of War and Peace at the bookmark.
I can't go on like this, he thought, *first thing tomorrow I'm going to make an appointment to see the doctor.*
The waiting room was crowded with men, women and children of all shapes, size and age; each of them coughing, sneezing and belching out their own particular strain of virus or bacteria.
Sebastian was convinced he could already feel the germs multiplying at a phenomenal rate inside his nasal passages. This would be followed, he imagined, by an overwhelming assault on his mucous membrane. By tomorrow night he feared he would be sitting at home tied to a box of tissues with his eyes and nose streaming. No chance of any sleep then.
He was just about to leave for the sanctuary of his home when the intercom System came to life and calmed him down.
Sebastian Orifice to room three please! It boomed.
By the time Sebastian entered the doctor's surgery Doctor Sheppard was already pulling on a pair of latex gloves.
"Right ... Drop your trousers, lie on the couch facing

the wall and tuck your knees up under your chin!" he barked imperiously.

"But doctor, I've come to see you about my insomnia."

"Oh ... OK, but in the meantime, drop your trousers, lie on the couch facing the wall and tuck your knees up under your chin ... I'm not wasting these latex gloves, they're expensive you know ... and they feel so smooth on your hands."

As Sebastian made his way home, he wondered if everybody could tell he was clenching his buttocks as he walked. He'd never had a great deal of faith in the ability of Dr Sheppard, but today was the icing on the cake. For a trained medical man to recommend counting sheep as a cure for insomnia was unbelievable. No pills, no prescription, just an old wives tale that every granny had told to her wide-eyed grandchildren for hundreds of years.

Yes, Sebastian thought, *He's got to go; I'll be changing my doctor soon, that's for sure.*

Sometime later, Sebastian was filled with dread as he sat watching the fading light through his living room window. He hated the night time, those long, eternal hours lying awake. It seemed to him, the rest of the world was gorging itself on refreshing sleep in preparation for the morrow's trials and tribulations, while he was being punished for some long forgotten sin.

Just after midnight, Sebastian thought he might as well go upstairs and try, yet again, for some sleep.

Once in bed he reached out for his book, and then stopped as something occurred to him.

Why do so many people talk about counting sheep? he mused, *I wonder if there's anything in it. I might as well just give it a try, after all, I've got nothing to lose.*

He turned out the light and conjured up in his mind a large, lush, green meadow. Proud of his realistic achievement, he scanned the green field and the horizon. It was then he noticed a hill in the middle of his imaginary field.

It looks like where the Teletubbies live, he thought. Almost immediately four strange shaped and strangely coloured creatures were scampering around on the hill. He tried to blot them out by imagining a flock of sheep grazing, but the creatures jumped on the sheep's backs and rode them around like miniature horses.

'What are their names now?' he asked himself, '*hmm, let me see, there's Laa Laa, Dipsy, Tinky Winky and errm, what's the other one, I can't think ... the little red one ... oh God what's his name?*'

He struggled on for a few minutes and then conceded defeat, *I give up, I'll look it up tomorrow.*

He lay in the dark until he could bear it no longer. It was too much for him to cope with. He suddenly sat bolt upright, turned on the bedside lamp and jumped out of bed.

Donning his dressing gown, he hurried downstairs, found his laptop computer and switched it on. Calling up his favourite search engine, he slowly

pecked at the keyboard with alternate index fingers, t-e-l-e t-u-b-b-i-e-s. The subtext of the first listing contained the names.
'Of course,' he sighed, *'Po'*.
As the tension drained away he closed the lid on the laptop and made his way back to bed.
Like a child playing with plasticine, he flattened the hill in the middle of his dreamscape field and banished the Teletubbies from his mind. Instead, he imagined a white picket fence enclosing a large area of the field forming a pen. He conjured up a gate in what he perceived to be the front of the enclosure and opened it. He looked around the field and imagined some sheep. Soon the whole virtual countryside was dotted with thousands of pure white sheep – he knew he probably wouldn't need this many but he didn't want to run the risk of running out when he was on the verge of falling asleep.
Within seconds the smiley faced, fluffy white sheep started to prance through the gate and he started counting. 'One, two, three, four, five,'
time passed,
'Six hundred and eighty-one, six hundred and eighty-two, six hundred and eighty-three, six hundred and eighty-four,'
more time passed,
'one thousand two hundred and fourteen, one thousand two hundred and fifteen, one thousand two hundred and sixteen ... I need a pee.'

He switched on the light yet again, opened the drawer on his bedside cabinet, took out a pen and small pad
and wrote down the number one thousand two hundred and sixteen, got up and made his way to the bathroom.
'I've got to admit I feel a bit tired,' he thought, 'perhaps it's working.'
Feeling better, he got back into bed, looked at the number on his pad to remind himself where he was up to and turned the light out. He closed his eyes and lay down. Once again he conjured up his imaginary field.
Suddenly, he screwed up his face in despair.
'Oh shit!' he wailed aloud, 'I've left the gate open,' 'Cum by, whistle, whistle, Cum by.'

VALENTINE

I have been dreading it for weeks! It has been lying in wait to ambush me. A ticking time bomb, hell bent on disrupting the serene, gentle flow of my life. Now it has arrived! This pervasive slot of time has invaded my bedroom, my house, my world.

The treacherous bedside clock has, yet again, imposed Valentine's Day upon my person whilst I slept. There is nothing I can do about it. My clock says it is the fourteenth of February, twenty-sixteen, and who am I to argue. This imperious timepiece has a direct radio link to a dictatorial master clock in the National Physical Laboratory which counts the vibrations of electrons in a caesium atom and claims to be accurate to one second within one-hundred and thirty-eight million years, whereas I have the remnants of a once highly efficient, albeit time blind, biological brain. No contest!

I could scream, rage and wave my arms about – even butt my head against the wall in anger if I had a mind to – but nothing would change. My vocal chords and my arms would be shifting Valentine's Day air. My futile, throbbing head would be butting a Valentine's Day wall. I'll just have to grit my teeth and get on with it.

Valentine's Day holds sad memories for me. It was the reason my partner and I split up.

We were both getting on a bit and decided we'd just

live together instead of getting married. We shared our lives for three blissful years, although each of these was punctuated by an unhappy Valentine's Day.

However much you love someone, it's difficult to express your true feelings in words. Even worse is when you try to embody your emotions within a present.

For our first Valentine's Day, I ordered a top-of-the-range set of stainless steel pans and gift wrapped them. The look on her face when she opened her present was enough to tell me I was lucky they hadn't become part of my gums.

Our second was no better. I took on board her controlled rage as, through gritted teeth, she gave me advice about incorporating some romance into Valentine's Day presents. I bought her pink, sexy underwear set, a suspender belt and some fishnet stockings.

"I'm sixty-seven years of age," she screeched, "don't think for one minute I'm gonna be prancing 'round the house in these you bloody pervert!"

Wrong again! Would I ever get it right?

She said my third attempt was the final straw.

"I've spent more than four grand on this," I protested.

All to no avail - she just continued packing her stuff. Her mind was made up. She was leaving me.

"Last year you said I should buy you a present more in line with our age group," I continued, hoping to change her mind.

She never spoke another word to me. She just finished her packing and slammed the door on the way out. I haven't heard from her from that day to this.

I decided I might as well keep the third present and use it myself. No point in wasting a luxury funeral plan with all the trimmings.

YOUNG LOVE

"I've never met anyone as tight as you, you grasping swine," Tracy hissed as she and her new boyfriend, Tommy, left the restaurant.
"Modern women don't like being paid for," Tommy said defending himself.
This annoyed Tracy even more.
"I'm not bothered about paying for myself but I didn't want to pay for you as well."
"I'm always skint at the end of the month. My wages don't go in 'till the first week."
"Then why ask me out on a date? You could have asked me when you got paid."
Tommy didn't reply. They walked on for a few minutes and Tracy hailed a cab.
"You're not wasting money on a cab are you?" Tommy asked. "It's only two miles."
Tracy stifled a scream. "Two miles in these heels, are you stupid?"
The cab pulled alongside and Tommy opened the door. Tracy quickly got in and as Tommy tried to follow her, she slammed the door behind herself and left him standing on the pavement. She called out her address to the driver and as the cab drove off, she wound down the window and popped her head out.
"It's only two miles," she grinned, "off you go."
"I think I've blown it with Tracy," Tommy said to his mate, Ronnie, the following evening.

Tommy and Ronnie had rubbed along together since they met in their first year at High School. Now, at twenty-three their relationship was more habitual than friendly.

"That must be a record, even for you," Ronnie teased, "to blow it on the first date. Not bad! What happened?"

"We went for a meal and I didn't have enough money to pay the bill."

"No change there then!"

"No, seriously. I thought we'd be going the pictures. I only had thirty quid, but she wanted to go for a meal. I said, 'OK, they do a good fish, chips and mushy peas at the Rose and Crown.' You should have seen the stare she gave me. I had to make out I was joking so I started laughing and asked her where she wanted to go."

"What did she say?"

"She said, 'let's go to the Golden Gourmet, they do Silver Service there.'"

"She was joking, right?"

Tommy puffed his cheeks out and shook his head from side to side.

"If you ask me Tom you're well out of it. She sounds high maintenance that one." Ronnie advised.

Tommy paused, then spoke. "The trouble is, I really fancy her, and I think she likes me, but now she thinks I'm tight with my money."

Ronnie gave a knowing laugh before he spoke.

"Listen, all's not lost. What we need to do is come up

with a plan that convinces her that you're not tight after all. Let's go for a pint and see what we can come up with."

Three hours and six pints later they had created and ironed out their master plan. Tommy would apologise to Tracy and take her on another date at the Golden Gourmet. This time he would have enough money on him to pay the bill, but during their conversation, around about the fourth pint, they had hit on a real gem of an idea to convince Tracy that Tommy was, in fact, a very generous person. Ronnie would get dressed up as a down and out. He would wear an old hoodie, just in case Tracy recognised him, and sit on the pavement somewhere outside the restaurant. Tommy would pretend to give him a large amount of money and gain favour with Tracy through his apparent generosity.

Tommy managed to grovel enough to convince Tracy to give him another chance. He picked her up in a cab and took her to the Golden Gourmet.

Having eventually managed to let go of his side of the pound coin he gave the cab driver as a tip, Tommy got out of the cab and scanned the pavement. Ronnie had done a good job. If Tommy hadn't known, he would never have recognised him.

"Good Lord," Tommy exclaimed loudly, look at that poor fellow over there. He must be freezing. Come on, we've got to help him."

He put his arm around Tracy and guided her over to where the man lay slumped against the wall.

"Here you are mate, this'll help you out," he said as he slowly counted out ten twenty pound notes, making sure that Tracy saw every one of them. He folded the money into a roll and handed it to the beggar who thanked him profusely.

Good voice Ron, Tommy thought, *but don't overdo it.*

As they walked the last few yards to the restaurant, Tracy pulled Tommy close and kissed him on the cheek.

"I had you wrong," she said, "sorry."

The meal was a huge success. They both tried lobster for the first time and washed it down with two excellent bottles of wine. Tommy bathed in Tracy's sparkling eyes and warm smile. He was surprised at her witty sense of humour. He was rapidly falling in love and he knew it.

At nine o'clock it was time to ring Ronnie and retrieve the two hundred pounds. Tommy stood up.

"Call of nature," he smiled at Tracy and made his way to the gents.

Once inside he dialled Ronnie on his mobile.

"Hi Ron."

"Hi Tom, how did the meal go?"

"Brilliant, I think she's falling for me, she's gorgeous."

"Sorry I couldn't make it, but it seems you didn't need me after all."

"What?"

"Nan had one of her turns. That's why I couldn't make it, but all's well that ends well eh!"

"But you *did* make it, I gave you the money."

"Oh no, don't tell me you gave the money to a real down and out? Oh mate, I'm so sorry."

Tommy staggered back to his seat in a daze; his mind was working overtime as he sat down without speaking. Tracy looked into his glazed eyes.

"What's up?" she asked.

He sat silent for a while then spoke.

"You're not gonna believe this Trace, but when I flushed the toilet, my wallet fell out of my pocket and went down the bog. Could you get the bill? I'll pay you back."

"I don't believe this, it's so embarrassing. It's your mess, you sort it out. I'm off home. Look, I think it's best if you don't call me again."

With that, she stormed out of the restaurant.

Tommy called the waiter.

"Can I have a word with the manager?" he whispered.

An hour or so later, Tracy lay on her bed chuckling to herself. Her mobile phone rang.

"Hi Ron," she giggled, "it worked a treat."

"No more than the tight git deserved," Ronnie said, "What shall we do with the money?"

"Let's have a slap-up meal at the Golden Gourmet."

"Why not," Ronnie agreed, "why not indeed."

IT WAS A GOOD YEAR

What an embarrassing day! The way they were all looking at me and judging me as I walked down the aisle. Even dad was a bit embarrassed. He never said so, but I could see it in his face. The fact that Tony, my husband to be was sixty-one, more than twice my age, was nobody's business but ours. By the time dad and I got to the altar I was trembling. I had heard some of the vicious, whispered comments as I passed through the congregation. Most of them based on our thirty-three year age difference and Tony's wealth.

The truth is, I've never been turned on by money, Tony's or anybody else's. What does turn me on though is the way he treats me like a lady. His ingrained good manners and consideration for other people. Add to that his well-toned muscles and stamina, due no doubt to his regular workouts at the gym, there's not much more a woman could ask for.

Before I met Tony, I dated a succession of men nearer to my own age, but there was always something missing. I think it was because they were always trying to prove themselves in some way or other, showing off, drinking too much, trying to prove how hard they were. It bored me rigid.

There was no way I could ever see myself marrying one of these insecure, overgrown schoolboys. Perhaps I expected too much of them!

Whatever the reason, I never formed any lasting

relationships and was beginning to think I'd missed the boat and would end up an old maid. Then I met Tony and my whole world changed. The first time he kissed me, my whole body tingled with excitement and pleasure. I knew he was the person I had been waiting to share my life with. As our love grew, I could sense that he wanted to ask me to marry him but was too shy because of our age difference. One evening, as we shared a bottle of wine, he suddenly blushed and popped the question. The hugs and kisses that followed gave him my answer.

My family and friends now accept Tony for what he is, a thoroughly decent person. I still get the occasional supposedly witty remarks though, about how much money we have, and silly jokes involving toilets and gold watches.

It's been just over three years since our wedding and we've never been happier. On our three-year anniversary, we got Sue, Tony's youngest daughter, to babysit the newest member of our family, Tony junior, and we went to a fabulous new restaurant.

We had our meal and afterwards Tony ordered a bottle of *Barbaresco Minuto fu Felice* 1949 vintage. I was amazed to discover that it cost him more than two hundred pounds. As we savoured its delightful flavour, he told me it had been bottled in the same year he was born.

"It was quite a good year for wine!" he told me.

"It was quite a good year for other things too," I replied.

THE SECRET DOOR

Simon looked at the door in dismay. Since the previous night, the hasp, staple and padlock - which he had almost sawn through with his virtual hacksaw - had gone. They had been replaced by a rotary three digit combination lock. The fact that the door had also changed colour didn't bother him, he was used to that, as it had happened so many times before. What did bother him though, was the fact that three digits meant one thousand possible combinations. This would be a doddle if he had enough time, but he never knew how much time he had left. He could look at his wristwatch and conjure up any time he wanted it to be, but it meant nothing in reality.

He figured that if he started with three zeros and allowed two seconds to set each combination and try the handle, it would take him just over thirty-three minutes to try every possible combination. If he was lucky it might even be one of the lower numbers – so much the better. Whichever way he looked at it, he now, at last, had a real opportunity to find out what was behind this accursed door.

He wondered what time it was in the real world. He had set his bedside alarm clock for 7am as usual, but this meant absolutely nothing during the course of a lucid dream.

One thing puzzled him greatly though. Through trial

and error he had learned to control every thought and event at will - until this door trespassed unbidden into his dreams.

Usually he was now so adept at controlling his dreams that he could spend his sleeping hours in the loving arms of top models and film stars, or spend huge lottery wins, but this door had put paid to all that. He was becoming obsessed.

He reached number 897 and was about to try the handle when his bedside alarm clock dragged him back into his drab, everyday life. "Bloody hell!" he muttered as he stretched then rubbed his eyes, "so near and yet so far."

He turned to face his snoring wife. She was much bigger than him and he reached up to put his arm around her. As he did so, he heard a familiar long, lingering rattling noise as a small cloud of methane gas escaped from her body. She stretched her arms out and knocked a glass of sterilising solution, which contained her false teeth, off the bedside cabinet and onto the bedroom carpet.

"Make me a cup of tea," she slurred.

Simon got out of bed, donned his dressing gown and headed downstairs to carry out her first order of the day. There would be others, a constant stream of them. There always was.

As the rest of the day unfolded, Simon was on autopilot.

The thoughts of his now regular nocturnal escapism preoccupied him and took over from the sheer drudgery of his normal daytime activities such as cleaning, washing up, cooking, and waiting hand and foot on his parasitic wife. He was determined to give himself every chance of success tonight. He decided that he would feign illness and go to bed early. In the meantime he would make a mental list of all the different challenges the door had presented since it imposed itself into his dreams.

"Tonight I'm gonna be prepared," he muttered.

The very fact that he heard himself utter the words made his confidence grow.

"Yes, tonight's the night!" he affirmed.

After what seemed to be the longest day of his life, it was time to put his plan into action, he told her he was feeling a bit under the weather and made his way up to the bedroom. Once in bed he found it difficult to sleep, but he realised this was due to the excitement that had been building up throughout the day, so he calmed himself down and waited.

Eventually he dozed off and began to dream. With a growing awareness he found himself floating towards the door. It always amazed him how rapidly he took control of each and every dream now. In the early, experimental days of his dream control, he found it difficult to steer the dream in the direction he wanted it to take. As soon as he became aware he was dreaming, the dream changed direction uncontrollably or he woke up.

Now, after much perseverance, he had learned how to take full control of his dreams without affecting them in other ways – apart from this blasted door.

He floated the last few virtual yards up to the door. He could hardly contain his joy. The three digit combination lock was still the only barrier. It had been reset to three zeros, but as he had reached 897 the previous night, Simon decided to work backwards. His trembling hands reset the tumblers to 999. It wasn't long before he reached 900 and he started to lose faith.

"Well, it's got to be one of the next two," he thought, "if not I'm never going to crack it, 899, no luck ... 898, no ... well that's it. I've had it."

Dejected, Simon wondered what he should do. This door thing had ruined the only pleasure in his life. Even if he steered the dream in another direction he could never fully enjoy himself the way he used to. He could never totally immerse himself without this strange, uninvited door niggling at the back of his mind. Then it suddenly occurred to him. Last night he had entered the 897 combination, but the alarm had woken him before he had time to try the handle. Not daring to believe, he entered the numbers, 8...9...7. He took a deep breath, turned the handle, and pulled the door.

Nothing happened, he pushed it. To his amazement the door moved slowly forward. He continued to push harder and the door swung fully open.

Beside himself with joy and relief, he stepped inside and looked around.

He was inside a large, dimly lit cavern. He walked a

few steps forward and started to explore. Suddenly he felt cold and a sense of abject fear pervaded his whole being. This was an irrational fear. A fear he remembered feeling as a child, during his most terrifying nightmares.

Then he heard it, the scurrying of hurried footsteps approaching from deep within the cavern. Too terrified to move, Simon was frozen to the spot as he watched a haggard, zombie-like figure, make its way to the open door. It paused and looked at him piteously as it crossed the threshold and disappeared into the dreamscape which Simon's mind had created. Immediately after, the door vanished and left a face of solid rocklike substance which blended with the rest of the cavern. A cavern which had now become Simon's prison.

As the ambulance rushed Simon's comatose body to St Mary's Hospital in Leeds, doctors at The Royal Hospital in Liverpool were examining a man who had unexpectedly woken up from a fifteen year coma. Although he kept hallucinating and raving about a cave and a locked door, he was expected to make a full recovery.

GOLDFINGER

I'll never forget that fateful day at the fair. My wife, Nell, said it was the only time our four children, Carlene, Denise, Jim and Carmen, had been quiet at the same time. They were lined up along the Hoopla Stall, not daring to breathe as I sized up the distant peg on which I hoped to hang my last remaining hoop.
They need not have worried. The high-pitched squeals of delight as the hoop found a new home said it all ... Nell and the children were quite pleased too.
The drive home was a nightmare. The children seemed to think that the one who shouted loudest got to name the newest addition to our family, a one-inch long goldfish.
After ten minutes or so of name-calling, bullying and cajoling that made a late session in the House of Commons seem like a church service, they finally decided he was a boy and settled on the name of Goldfinger.
Then came talk of the christening.
"How can you christen a fish when its head's under the water all the time?" asked Carlene.
"Easy", replied Jimmy, "just get a straw and blow air on its head."
Little did I know as we made our way home with our prize that our lives would never be the same again.

The first hurdle we had to overcome was to arrange bed and breakfast for Goldfinger, followed by more permanent accommodation. As the kids chatted wildly about ponds and the development of an expensive aquarium, I racked my brains trying to remember if that old chipped pudding basin was still tucked away at the back of the kitchen cupboard.

After much pouting and sulking on both sides, we compromised and agreed on a bowl from the pet shop. I knew of course that this was a total waste of money, as these fish never seem to survive very long anyway.

Six months later, I was forced to agree how cruel it was to keep a fish as large as Goldfinger in such a small bowl. Something would have to be done.

As Nell massaged a soothing balm into my aching back, I wondered if the pond I'd just finished digging really did have to be that big, or were the kids just pulling my leg.

We installed Goldfinger in his new home and watched as he made full use of his fins and tail for the first time in months. The kids sat round the pond until it was dark, their faces strained from scowling at any bird that dared to land in our back garden - there would be no more leftover toast for *them*!

The world took a few more turns taking us into late November. Then one weekend the tranquillity of our usual Saturday morning lie-in was shattered. Nell and I were awakened by the cries of four panic-stricken children. I was pulled, half dressed, down the stairs and out into the back garden to the shores of our huge pond. I looked down and saw Goldfinger leisurely swimming around ... under a thin layer of ice.

On our way to the pet shop, I wondered if there had been anything else I could have said to convince the kids that goldfish don't feel the cold.

That was over twenty years ago and Goldfinger is now a seven-inch long giant in goldfish terms.

As for me, I'm more than twenty years older myself, and each month as my creaking frame struggles to change the water in Goldfinger's three-foot-long tank, I wonder why none of my now grown-up children fought for custody as, one by one, they flew the nest and moved into their own homes.

PREMONITIONS

It was 31st of October 2017 and Michael was sweating with the fear of a condemned prisoner awaiting execution. If his bad dream was to come true, he only had one day to live.

He wished he had not told his wife, Molly, now. She had made the last seventeen days hell. Molly knew how superstitious he was and she still carried on. Her wicked sense of humour was being stretched to the full and he was totally fed up with her constant mocking laughter. He used to like the sound of her laughter as they shared a rude joke or two, it seemed to enhance the humour, but now it was just a raucous, guttural cackle that grated on his already frayed nerves.

He thought back to the morning when he had told her. It was a Bright sunny morning. Saturday, October 14th 2017, to be precise, the date was etched in his memory. It had held the promise of a relaxing weekend and they were both in good spirits as they savoured their full English breakfast and read the morning papers.

"I had a weird dream last night!" Michael suddenly announced.

Molly grunted her acknowledgement without taking her eyes off the paper.

"I dreamt I died in my sleep on Halloween night," he continued.

Molly's interest sprung to life as she lowered her paper and stared him in the eye.

"Ooh!" she said, "you shouldn't have told me, you shouldn't tell *anyone*."

"Don't be daft," he argued. "Why not?"

She leaned across the table toward him, pulled her most frightening face, and hissed,

"Friday night's dream if on Saturday told, is sure to come true no matter how old."

She laughed as she watched the blood drain from his face.

"That's stupid; you've just made that up," he said as he effected a little laugh of bravado.

"Google it!" she replied bluntly, "and don't forget ... it was Friday the thirteenth yesterday."

Their breakfast continued in silence.

As Molly put the dishes into the dishwasher, she peeped through the door and chuckled to herself as she saw Michael frantically booting up the laptop. She made two cups of instant coffee and took them into the lounge where Michael was staring blankly at the computer screen.

"You didn't make it up," he said. "It's on the net."

Molly could not miss such an opportunity to fan the flames of his fear.

"So if your dream *does* come true, counting today, you've got eighteen more days to live! I'll just go and mark it on the calendar."

She put down the coffee and went into the hall where their calendar hung on a small notice board.

Speaking aloud in a mocking tone, she called back, "Eighteen days left, and that's counting today."

Much to Michael's consternation, she did the same thing every day, counting down with the enthusiasm of a child removing the daily chocolate reward from an advent calendar - each time with the same cackling laugh he had grown to hate.

He wrenched his thoughts back to the present. "Could this really be my last day?" he asked himself aloud.

He made a cup of coffee with four heaped teaspoons of strong instant and took two more caffeine tablets.

There's no way I'm going to sleep tonight, he thought, *if I stay awake my dream can't come true.*

The day seemed to be an eternity as he watched with dread the setting of the pale, late October sun. The evening closed in on him like a dark shroud. High on caffeine, he was extremely edgy and shuddered nervously as the television displayed the usual Halloween horrors from ghostly pumpkins, witches, and the films, *Nightmare on Elm Street* and *Friday the Thirteenth Part Two.*

Just after twelve midnight, Molly tried in vain to convince Michael that as it was now November 1st, Halloween was over for another year and he was safe. Michael remained unconvinced.

Unable to take any more, Molly went to bed leaving him sitting wide eyed on the sofa. He made himself another strong coffee and took two more tablets. He turned the sound up on the television to stop himself from nodding off, and launched into the Times Crossword. He was determined - there was no way he was going to sleep tonight.

The swishing of the lounge curtains woke him up as the low November sun shone through the window and onto his face.

"Fancy leaving the telly on all night," Molly complained, "and so loud, what will the neighbours think?"

Michael did not care. He had made it. Although he had a severe headache from all the caffeine he had swallowed, it did not bother him at all. He could hear the birds singing and he was alive. It truly was a glorious morning.

"I've made it," he said in sheer jubilation, "I've made it!"

"Hang on," Molly said mischievously, "who said it would be this year?"

She walked out into the hall and shouted aloud as she wrote on the calendar, "The first of November, 365 days left ... and that's counting today."

Michael cringed as her cackling laughter echoed throughout their home.

SEDUCTION

Simon knew he shouldn't have agreed to meet Lulu but he had to put a stop to her stalking him. His new wife, Sally, would be furious if she knew about the way Lulu followed him everywhere. She already hated Lulu, and with good reason.

Although Simon and Lulu were divorced long before Sally met Simon, Lulu just couldn't let go. She had long since remarried but still put every obstacle in the way of Simon's happiness.

The meeting, just like all the others, was a complete waste of time, it seemed the only way to be rid of Lulu was to sell up and move out of town. After weeks of promises and persuasion, he finally convinced Sally to move. They sold their house in Liverpool and moved to Ilfracombe, Devon.

The move was quite an upheaval and it took a while for them to settle in. They both missed their friends and family, but eventually, their new place started to feel like home and they started to relax a bit more. It was only now they became aware of how much Lulu had been ruining their lives with her interference. They both agreed that they should put the whole sorry episode out of their minds.

"The past is the past, so why should we let it continue to cause us grief?" Simon said in one of his alcohol fuelled philosophic moments.

"Too true," agreed Sally, who was sharing his

twelve-year-old whisky.

Imagine their horror when a removal van pulled up outside a vacant house opposite and Lulu, followed obediently by her puppet-like husband, disembarked. Sally howled like a banshee all day long, while Simon paced from room to room thanking God that they didn't own a pet rabbit.

It didn't take long for Lulu to make her approach. Having sent her zombie husband off to the local job centre, she crossed over the narrow road and knocked on Simon and Sally's door.

"I need help," she said to Simon as soon as they opened the door. They both gazed at her as she stood there in her short flared pink skirt and see-through top. There was no denying her beauty, but to dress like this at 10am smacked of sheer desperation.

"Can you come over and help me to move some furniture?" she continued.

Simon and Sally looked at each other in disbelief.

"I can spare you about ten minutes," replied Simon reluctantly.

"I'll come too," Sally said, trying hard not to show her anger. There was no way she was going to leave Simon alone with Lulu.

While they were working, Lulu made sure that she bent down and climbed at every opportunity, displaying her skimpy knickers as much as possible. Top of the bill was when she allowed her left breast to pop out and become visible through her see-through top. Sally and Simon were both hot and flustered, and it wasn't just from moving the furniture.

Over the next few days Sally and Simon were given a private fashion parade of the sexiest clothes in Lulu's extensive wardrobe. Simon felt deeply guilty and ashamed about his growing desire to bed his ex-wife once again. He knew he was betraying Sally with his thoughts and tried to console himself with the thought that any normal man would fancy Lulu. He wondered if Sally had guessed his guilty secret – she seemed a bit cool towards him lately. *I'll make it up to her*, he thought. *I'll pay her some special attention tonight.*

That evening, he sat her in front of the television and told her to relax. He clattered about in the kitchen for an hour or so, then brought in a tray containing a plate of spaghetti bolognaise and a large glass of wine. He continued to pamper her for the rest of the evening and by bedtime they were both feeling very mellow indeed. Once they were in bed, Simon kissed her shoulder and rolled over to cuddle her. He cried out as something sharp scratched his side. Pulling back the sheets, he picked up an unusual and obviously expensive gold earring.

"I don't remember you wearing these," he said. "When did you get them?"

Sally blushed bright red and began to cry. "They're Lulu's," she replied. "I'm sorry, I wanted to tell you but I don't understand it myself. I've never felt that way about another woman before."

THE PAIN

"If you don't put your foot down I'll be having it in the car ... Agggh."
"Will you stop screaming Cassie, I'm trying to drive. The way you're carrying on you'd think you're the first woman to have a baby. It can't be hurting that much!"
"How would you know you stupid bugger, agggh, just hurry up will you?"
"Well shut up and stop your whining. Do that silly breathing thing you told me about."
 An angry silence descended on the car's interior as both passenger and driver stared blankly ahead. Cassie tried to control the intensity of her labour pains and held both hands over her mouth in an effort to stifle her cries, in doing so, she screwed up and contorted her face in accordance with whatever level of pain she was trying to deny. At the same time, she puffed her cheeks up and down like a trumpeter trying to blow a note on a blocked trumpet. Sam threw a sideways glance and burst into a fit of laughter.
"You heartless swine," Cassie screamed. "Don't you realise how much pain I'm in?"
"I thought you were practising for a gurning competition," laughed Sam, almost losing control of the car.
 Sam pulled up sharply in the maternity unit car

park, ambled slowly around to the passenger side and opened the car door. Cassie swallowed her desire for independence and reluctantly clung on to Sam's arm and shoulder, easing herself out of the car. Between them, they shuffled their way through the large revolving door and into the reception area where they met Cassie's mum, Margaret, who had been waiting anxiously since she got the phone call telling her that she was likely to be a Gran by the end of the day.

"Are you sure you won't change your mind?" Cassie said softly to Sam, "I'd really like you to be present at the birth. They say it creates a better bond with the baby."

"Sod that for a game of soldiers!" Sam replied sharply. "I'll be in the Red Lion across the road wetting the baby's head. You've got your mum now haven't you? You don't need me anymore. Just give me a ring on your mobile when you've had it."

Sam noticed that Cassie's eyes were filling up and her lower lip was beginning to quiver.

"Look Cass, you wanted this baby, not me. I only went along with it to make you happy – to satisfy your maternal instincts. As far as I'm concerned we've got a good relationship as we are. We've been together for seven and a half years; surely that says something? We've been able to go on holidays any time the mood took us, go for a night out at the drop of a hat whenever we felt like.

Now that's all going to change. We'll need

babysitters to go anywhere together, all that nappy and bottle stuff, sleepless nights, you too tired to enjoy yourself anymore. I really can't understand why anyone would want to blight their lives with a baby. I'm sorry, it's just not me!"

Lecture over, Sam was gracious enough to see Cassie to her room in the Maternity Unit and help her unpack, but Cassie could see that Sam just didn't want to be there. Within a few minutes of finishing the unpacking, the call of the pub proved too strong, and after giving Cassie a dutiful peck on the cheek and openly flirting with the pretty young nurses, Sam made a quick exit to the pub.

Cassie's mum screwed up her face in disgust.
"I'm sorry, and I know you don't want to hear this right now, but I don't know what you see in that horrible swine!"
Cassie didn't answer, she just bowed her head. Deep down inside she knew her mum was right.

Four torturous hours later, Cassie cuddled her son. At eight pounds four ounces, he had announced his healthy entrance into the world with a powerful cry that promised a strong life ahead of him. Once bathed and fed, he slept deeply and began the twenty year plus process of growing.

Cassie twisted and turned on the pillows that were propping her up in an effort to get comfortable. Her eyes filled with tears and Margaret took hold of her hand and squeezed it lovingly.
"You'll feel better soon, love. Your emotions are all

over the place at the moment, bound to be!"

"It's not that mum,' she cried, 'I'm just wondering what will happen if Sam doesn't bond with the baby. Our life together could be ruined. It might even split us up."

If only, Margaret thought. Then she spoke.

"Are you still going to call him Samuel?"

"Yes mum, I've told you. Now will you stop going on about it?"

"It's such an old fashioned name though. Why don't you call him Michael after your dad? He was a good man. Perhaps it's just as well he's no longer here to see how badly Sam treats you. He wouldn't have stood for it I can tell you. If he'd seen..."

Cassie interrupted her mother mid sentence.

"Mum, I've just had a baby, the last thing I want to hear is you raking all this up again."

"I'm sorry love," Margaret replied, "it's just that I want what's best for you, that's all."

Their conversation ended as Cassie's sister, Susan, came in carrying a basket of fruit and a box of chocolates with a card attached. She leaned over, placed her gifts on the bedside cabinet and kissed her sister on the cheek.

"Hi Cass, you OK?" she asked.

"The Midwife said I'll be fine in a few days," Cassie replied, "but at the moment I feel as though I'll never be able to sit down and relax again - ever."

Susan said hello to her mother then scanned the small maternity room.

"Where's your useless other half?" she said to Cassie. "Don't you start Sue," Cassie objected, "I've just had all that off mum ... and will you stop calling her that. Her name's Samantha. She's in the Red Lion across the road wetting the baby's head."

THE HOODIE

Susan tried yet again to open the bedroom door; it was still locked.
"I've done you something to eat," she shouted through the wooden panels.
She waited for a while but there was no reply.
"Suit yourself," she murmured, making her way downstairs to the kitchen where two meals were laid out on the dining table.
She looked at her plate of steak, onion gravy and mashed potato and decided she no longer felt hungry. She put the two untouched meals into the oven.
Maybe we'll both feel a bit more like eating later on, she thought.
 Making her way into the lounge, she succumbed to the magnetic pull of the drinks cabinet and poured herself a large vodka and diet coke.
She sat down on the sofa, put her drink on the coffee table and scowled at the crumpled Hoodie that lay on the hearthrug. Her mind replayed the image of Peter, her son, raging as he lashed it to the floor before stamping up to his room.
When she told him he wasn't allowed wear it there had been a blazing row, he accused her of being a snob and trying to take over his life.
 It wasn't as though she failed to understand his point of view. When all said and done Peter was

right, it *was* only a jacket with a hood attached. The problem is that others wouldn't look at it like that. No, if he was allowed to wear it, then he'd be ranked the same as certain youngsters who roamed the estate getting up to mischief and causing trouble.

When she and her husband, Tom, had first moved onto the estate, it had been very quiet and the majority of the residents were nice, polite people. Over the years however, a lot of the nice families had moved out and been replaced with people who were less responsible. Some of the teenagers had grown up lacking in parental guidance and this had led to a fall in standards. There were now gangs of youths who roamed the estate causing trouble. They hid their identities by wearing Hoodies similar to the one Peter wanted to wear.

Peter wasn't like that of course - he was a well behaved, polite boy. Susan was extremely proud of him and normally trusted his judgment, but at fourteen he was still very impressionable, and she didn't want him mixing with the wrong type of people.

She took a large swig of her vodka and coke and leaned back into the soft, red cushions of her leather chesterfield.

A short time later, she heard Peter open his bedroom door and make his way down the stairs.

"I'm sorry I lost my temper Mum," he said softly, "I won't wear it again."

He picked up the Hoodie and handed it to her.

"Do you want a cup of tea?"

"No thanks," Susan smiled, "I've already got a drink, just make one for yourself."

She watched him as he walked out into the kitchen, amazed how tall and good-looking he'd become. With his sun-streaked fair hair and deep blue eyes, he was the spitting image of Tom.

If only Tom could see him now, she thought as her eyes moistened, *he'd be so proud.*

She dabbed her eyes and took another sip of her drink. It was now more than twelve years since Tom had died.

She drained her glass and looked down at the Hoodie. As much as she hated the thing, it meant so much to Peter that she couldn't bring herself to throw it out.

I'll put it somewhere safe and give it back to him when he's old enough to know better, she thought. She took it up to her bedroom, opened the little-used drawer at the bottom of her wardrobe and stuffed the Hoodie at the back. As Susan closed the drawer, she caught sight an old biscuit tin in which she kept some keepsakes. Still thinking of Tom, she took out the tin, sat on her bed, and opened it.

She took out some old black and white photographs and slowly thumbed through them. Lingering on one of the snapshots she smiled warmly, it was a picture of herself and Tom taken during a day out at Blackpool when they were in their late teens. It showed them sitting astride Tom's

Lambretta scooter, both dressed in their Mod gear. Tom was wearing a collarless jacket over a turtleneck sweater and a pair of huge Chelsea boots. Susan wore a *Mary Quant* style dress and a beret. Later that day, as they sat on the beach and watched the setting sun, Tom had told her how much he loved her and asked her to marry him.

"How silly we must have looked," she said aloud with a laugh.

She remembered how her mum used to worry about the way they dressed because of the fighting between Mods and Rockers.

"It's not what you wear that matters Mum," she used to reply, "but what's in your heart."

A sudden awareness swept over her. She hurriedly put the photographs back into the tin, retrieved the Hoodie from the wardrobe drawer, and made her way downstairs to where Peter sat watching television. He stared in bewilderment as she squeezed next to him on his armchair, placed the Hoodie loosely around his shoulders and kissed him on the cheek. Peter blushed a bright shade of red.

"Mu...um," he laughed, "you've flipped."

THE JOURNEY

Peter squeezed Pat's hand but she hardly felt it. She looked down at his frail body. He'd lost so much weight he was indistinguishable from the crumpled bedding. She remembered how big he had always been, and how he'd struggled with his diet plans and his weight throughout their forty-five years of marriage. She tried to control her sobs as tears flooded down her cheeks and dripped onto Peter's bony forearm. He opened his eyes and struggled to turn his head towards her.
"Don't cry sweetheart," he said softly, "all my suffering will be over soon. I'm going on the biggest journey anyone can make. I know it's a one-way ticket but it could still be a great adventure, now wipe those tears and give me a kiss."
She leaned over the bed and kissed him. He smiled and closed his eyes for the last time.
"Hello Peter." Peter suddenly became aware of his father's presence. "I've come to guide you. You did well son!"
"I can't see you dad," Peter said.
"You will in a while son - when you adjust. You have no physical body now and can no longer rely on your six senses."
"Six?" Peter asked in surprise.
"Yes, the sixth sense did exist in your old form but as mankind relied so heavily on sight, touch, hearing,

smell and taste, it played very little part in further evolution and declined. We have different ways of interfacing with this plane of existence. For me to try to explain would be a waste of time. You are undergoing a transition; in the meantime, your essence will still try to align your thinking and awareness with your old perceptions. When your new senses adapt you'll be amazed at the things you can do."

"How many senses will I have?"

"As many as you need or want."

"How am I communicating with you now?"

"I have the ability to communicate with any life form, as you soon will."

"I can't believe all this is really happening. A new existence, a new beginning, how can this be?"

"Well, the best way I can answer that is to ask, what's more unbelievable than the life you've just left? Anyway, I'll leave you now while you continue the process of your regeneration. The next time we meet you will be more able to cope with your new environment. It will not take you long to realise that we are omnipotent gods, capable of anything you can imagine. Mum will be in touch soon, she knows you're here, and when Pat and the children pass over, we'll be here to welcome them. Goodbye for now."

"Goodbye Dad, I'm so pleased were all going to be together again. To think, all my life I feared death and it's turned out to be the best thing that ever happened to me!"

With that thought, the residual oxygen from Peter's last breath was used up by his dying brain. As the synaptic connections that had created his consciousness started to disintegrate and decompose, his last dream ended.

Peter slipped into the dark, perpetual abyss that was his death.

ALONE

The seagulls and cormorants rose in scattered panic as the drone of the helicopter became too much for them to bear. It had surprised them as it suddenly appeared from a blanket of low grey cloud. It swept low along the beach up to a grassy area just beyond the dunes and inched its way down. It hovered about three feet from the ground. After a short while, the cabin door slid open and two large bags came flying out. They were followed by the figure of a man who battled against the downdraught from the rotors as he turned and waved his thanks to the pilot. Within seconds, the helicopter had risen again and disappeared into the grey woollen blanket that was the sky.

Tim Brewer looked all around him. He had made a good choice. For the next week, the small, uninhabited island of Scaravay, in the Outer Hebrides was to be his home. Although it had cost him a lot of money it was going to be worth it. He did a slow three-sixty degree turn surveying the tiny forty-acre island and was pleased with the utter desolation he perceived.

Nobody, apart from Geoff Spice, a Merchant Banker who had agreed to be cast away on here for a month in order to give up smoking, had lived on this island since the highland clearances of the eighteenth and nineteenth centuries.

He wouldn't be bothered by tourists or sightseers here. It was perfect.

He smiled as he remembered a bit of banter he had with his friend Mike Crean just before he left for the island. Mike had jokingly suggested that after a week in solitary confinement, Tim might find the few remaining wild sheep too much of a temptation. Picking up his bags, he made his way inland towards a small rocky crag near the centre of the island. This was a good place to pitch his tent and it would give him some shelter from the wind.

As he set up camp, Tim's mind drifted back home and he recalled the heated conversations he had with his wife and two teenage daughters. They just didn't understand and nothing he said made them see sense. He'd even invited them to come along with him and suggested to his wife that a week of relative deprivation would be good for their ever more materialistic daughters.

By the evening of the sixth day, Tim was losing his nerve and beginning to have some doubts. Perhaps his wife and daughters had been right to argue against such a trip. He had never felt so isolated in his life. He always thought he would cope well with being alone, but this was a different kind of alone.

He looked at his watch so often on the first day that he decided to take it off his wrist and hide it in the tent.

The nights were even worse! He dreaded the evening twilight, knowing that he was in for another cold, endless stretch of half-sleep which left him physically drained for the following day.

Then there was the intense, palpable darkness. The ideal medium to invoke his primeval fears.

Fears he would have laughed at in the security of his bedroom at home. But now he was ashamed. The long neglected childhood monsters and ghosts which had been buried deep in his subconscious mind were now paying him nightly visits. He could well understand why so many ancient tribes paid homage to the rising sun.

The seventh day was yet another eternity, the only comfort being that after enduring one more night, the helicopter would be arriving to transport him back to the reality of everyday life. The general hustle and bustle and the inane jabber of his wife and daughters seemed so attractive to him now.

The long day eventually drew to its close and Tim shivered as he settled down in his sleeping bag. Just as he was about to nod off, he was startled by a regular crunching noise outside the tent. He froze and strained to listen more carefully. There was no doubt about it – somebody, or something was walking about outside the tent. Eyes wide with fear, Tim curled himself into a ball and, as beads of cold sweat began to form down his back and on his forehead, he started to recite the Lord's Prayer under his breath.

There was no police force or emergency services here. You could scream as loud as you liked, but no one would hear you. No one would come to your aid. For the rest of the night Tim lay there counting the seconds, each one taking him a tiny step further towards the sanctuary of dawn. In those few agonising hours, Tim learned what most of us never learn in a whole lifetime, the true meaning of the word *alone*.

He was still lying wide awake with fear as the inside of the tent canvas lit up with the morning light. He listened to the reassuring noises of the seabirds as they set about seeking out their breakfast. His courage now restored with the early morning sunlight, he decided to have a look outside the tent. Carefully, he pulled down the zip to the opening and popped his head out. All was quiet. He climbed out of the tent and had a look around. In the gap between the base of the crag and his tent, lay an old bedraggled sheep sheltering from the wind. Tim laughed aloud, partly with relief and partly with the shame of being so afraid. He was not the man he thought he was. He had learned a lot about himself in the past week.

As he boarded the helicopter three hours later, Tim tried to play down the week's events in his own head, but as much as he tried, he couldn't deny that the trip had cost him dearly, both financially and emotionally.

It had been worth it though, worth every penny to avoid witnessing the nauseous extravagance of yet another royal wedding.

IN THOUGHT, WORD AND DEED

Joe smiled warmly as he looked into Amanda's bright blue eyes. He kissed her affectionately on the cheek and slowly undid the buttons of her pale pink see-through top. He peeled it back over her perfect shoulders and gazed at her black lace bra.

"You're so beautiful," he whispered. "If only Sally was half as good looking, I'd be a very lucky man."

He felt himself flush with shame as soon as the words left his lips.

The last thing he wanted was to betray his wife, Sally, but they had been married for nearly twenty years now and, although it filled him guilt, he had come to expect the odd disloyal thought now and again.

He wondered if Sally ever had similar thoughts. Had *she* looked longingly at other men and admired their looks and figure? Had *she* ever wondered what it would be like to spend the night with somebody else?

He tried to make himself feel better by recounting all the times she'd drooled over Cliff on the television.

I'll bet if she ever got the chance to go out with him she'd jump at it, he thought.

Deep down inside however, he knew he was just kidding himself.

All he could say for certain was that Sally had always put him and the kids first. She was one of the most unselfish and considerate people he had ever known. This made him feel even more guilty so he tried to push all thoughts of Sally from his mind.

He let go of Amanda's pink top and watched it float to the floor as he fumbled awkwardly with the tight waistband of her short, pleated skirt. He finally managed to undo the zip and the skirt slid over her smooth hips and lay in a crumpled heap around her ankles.

The fact that Amanda wasn't wearing any knickers didn't surprise him. He knew that she was only wearing a bra because she had a see-through top on. He stood back so that he could admire Amanda's overall beauty. He was besotted with her, and try as he might, there seemed to be nothing he could do about it.

He caught sight of his well-worn wedding ring and once again his thoughts returned to Sally. He could remember when her figure was almost as beautiful as Amanda's and she too could wear such fashionable clothes. Not any more though, thanks to giving birth to their four children and a generous helping of middle age spread.

He tried to guess Amanda's age as he gently put his arms around her and unhooked her bra. She looked about twenty-five but he knew she was a lot older than that.

As Joe carefully folded Amanda's bra he heard the swish of a curtain rail and turned to see the angry face of Mr. Allen, the manager of the Ladies Fashion

Department.

"Come on Joe," he barked, "what's keeping you? ... It's twenty to nine and we've got two more window displays to finish."

BARRICADE

Mick Delaney put a box of groceries down on the step and fumbled in his jacket pocket for his keys. As he opened the front door, he felt the stress and strain of the day start to melt away. Picking up the box, he made his way into the sanctuary of his flat.
What a day, he thought as he placed his box on the kitchen table. *There's that much traffic on the roads these days it won't be worth going to work soon.*
Mick thought back to when he first became a Private Hire Taxi Driver in Liverpool. That was twelve years ago when the roads were less crowded. You could make a good living then if you worked hard, but now the roads were jam-packed all day long, especially around the Pier Head and the Albert Dock area.
He unpacked his box then rewarded himself with a cup of instant coffee which he took into the lounge. He turned on the television just in time for the late afternoon news. After a few minutes of scowling at unfolding world events, Mick caught the scent of something alien to his lounge and glanced around. He did a double take on a vase of flowers standing proudly on top of his bookcase in the alcove.
"Oh no," he said out loud, "I knew I shouldn't have given her that key!"
Susie Ellison walked happily across the school playground towards the gate.
She was thoroughly enjoying her first year as a fully

qualified Primary School teacher, but today she had not been able to concentrate properly and was glad to be going home. She smiled as she wondered how her boyfriend Mick would react to the flowers and the card she had left in his flat at lunchtime. It was the first anniversary of the day they met and she wanted to celebrate it in style, perhaps with a meal at their favourite restaurant, or something equally enjoyable.

Mum had asked her to pick up a few bits and pieces on the way home so she headed for the high street. After that it would be shower, glam up, and round to Mick's flat. She couldn't wait to see him and find out if he'd remembered. *Maybe he's even bought me a present*, she thought,

perhaps a small present in a tiny box with a diamond cluster on it. She giggled loudly, then blushed as she saw a small group of her pupils were grinning at her.

Back at Mick's flat, he tore open the envelope that had lain next to the flowers and examined the card it contained. His heart sank as he read Susie's heartfelt words of love. It suddenly became clear that she cared for him far more than he realised.

I'm not ready for this, he thought, *and I don't think I ever will be!*

Susie tried the key for a second time, but the lock still would not turn. She rang the bell and waited for Mick to open the door. She threw her arms around him and kissed him full on the lips.

"My key's stopped working," she said. "I'll have to get another one cut."

Mick did not reply. He just turned and walked in ahead of her.

"Coffee?" he asked.

"Yes please, I'd love one ... are you OK?"

"I'm fine," he replied, "it's just that there are one or two things we need to sort out."

"Sort out?" Susie quizzed.

"Well, for one thing, I need more space," Mick asserted.

Susie could not believe her ears.

"More space?"

"Will you stop repeating everything I say," snapped Mick, "you sound like a parrot."

"Well if you stop talking in riddles and say what you mean then perhaps I won't have to."

She's right, Mick thought, *how could she know what I've been thinking about all afternoon.*

"Things are moving too fast," he said aloud, "I feel as though I have no time to myself."

There was an awkward silence. Then Susie spoke.

"You put the snib on the door didn't you?" she said, "*that's* why my key wouldn't work."

Mick didn't answer. He just stared at the floor uncomfortably.

"You had no need to do that. All you needed to do was to ask me to give it back."

She twisted the key off her key ring and banged it loudly onto the table.

"I don't think I'll bother with the coffee if it's all the same to you," she shouted as she stormed out, "you can have all the space you want."

Later that evening, Susie leaned over the side of her bed and threw another damp tissue into the wastepaper basket. She had been determined not to cry, but the disappointment had been too much for her to take. She thought how happy she had been in this very room less than three hours earlier as she sat in front of her dressing table mirror doing her make-up and her hair.

How could he have treated me like that? she thought, *in the year we've been together we haven't had one row, then all of a sudden, this!*

There was a knock on Susie's bedroom door.

"I've made you a cup of tea love. Can I come in?" Without waiting for an answer, Susie's mum, Miranda, opened the door and came in carrying a tray. "I've made you a nice ham sandwich too. You'll feel better when you've had something to eat."

"Thanks mum," Susie said with a sob, "but I'm not hungry."

Miranda welled up as she looked into Susie's mascara covered face. She knew her daughter wasn't quick to tears. Something, or somebody, must have really upset her.

"Was it Mick?" Miranda asked.

Susie nodded slowly as the tears started flowing again.

"He said he needed more space," she sobbed.

"I knew it!" Miranda said as she put her arms around Susie and cuddled her.

She had never really taken to Mick. It wasn't just the age gap. The fact that at 38 Mick was 16 years older than Susie *did* bother her, but it wasn't just that, there was something else. Although Mick was normally very well mannered and every inch a gentleman, there was something lurking under the surface. Something Miranda couldn't quite put her finger on.

Miranda pushed a cup of tea into Susie's hands. "Drink some tea love, you'll feel better."

Susie gazed blankly ahead and sipped the tea.

"I'm going 'round to see him!" Miranda went on, "there's something not quite right and I'm going to find out what it is."

"No, just leave it mum, don't get involved." Susie said half-heartedly, "it'll only make things worse!"

"You're sitting on your bed crying your eyes out. I don't think I can make things *much* worse. Do you?" asked Miranda.

Susie didn't answer.

Mick opened the door and was totally shocked to see Miranda standing on his doorstep.

"I ... I thought it was Susie," he stammered.

"Aren't you going to invite me in?" she goaded.

"Of course, I'm sorry, come in Miranda." he replied.

He held back the door and gestured for her to go first.

"I suppose you know that Susie's distraught at home. She can't stop crying. What have you done to her?"

"I haven't done anything to speak of," Mick said, "I

put the snib on the door, that's all."
"That's all? So after giving her a key you decided to lock her out. How is she supposed to know where she stands?"
"It's complicated," Mick replied.
"Well, tell me about it," Miranda said sitting down, "Let's make it uncomplicated."
Mick paused and took a deep breath to calm himself. "Susie's the first girl I've felt anything for since..." he paused and took another breath, "I suppose I'd better start at the beginning."
"As good a place as any," quipped Miranda.
"When I was still in the third year at school, I fell for one of my classmates. I was totally in love with her and she said she was in love with me. Both our parents used to laugh about it and said we were 'infatuated' with each other. Well this 'infatuation' stood the test of time and for the next ten years we were inseparable. Next thing, she was gone."
"What happened to her?" Miranda interrupted.
"We got engaged, that's what happened to her. Once she put the ring on her finger she changed completely. She said it made her feel trapped. She was seeing less and less of me and more of her friends. Then on one occasion, when she returned from a holiday in Spain, I was so looking forward to seeing her but when we met up she told me ..." he paused.
"What?" said Miranda impatiently, "she told you what?"

Mick bowed his head. "She told me she needed more space, then within a few months she married someone she'd met in Spain."

Mick suddenly became aware of what he'd done. How he'd blocked out Susie's love to protect himself from being hurt again. He felt as though his emotional dam had been breached as all the pent up love he had for Susie flooded into him.

"What a fool I've been Miranda!" he said, "what a fool."

Miranda was convinced she'd seen Mick change right there and then before her eyes. He had softened visibly and was so full of remorse that she felt sorry for him. She now understood why she felt the way she did about Mick. The emotional barrier he built up over the years had kept everybody, except Susie, at arm's length.

Susie frowned as she heard another knock on her bedroom door. She really didn't want to be bothered with anything, but she wanted to know what Mick had been saying to her mum.

"Come in mum," she shouted, "what did he say?"

She gasped in amazement as the door opened and Miranda came in closely followed by a solemn faced Mick. He walked over to where she was sitting on her bed and knelt down on one knee.

"Susie," he said, "please forgive me, I've been such a fool. I know we've only been together for twelve months, but I love you so much. Will you marry me?"

INVISIBILITY

John's trembling hands struggled to open his newly delivered parcel. He had been restlessly pacing his front room-cum-laboratory waiting for the postman to deliver the final part of his latest scientific project and now it had finally arrived. He managed to make a tear in the tough, special delivery plastic paper and remove the small cardboard box which contained the key to a better future. He opened the box and removed the programmable quad processor chip with his antistatic tweezers and placed it on the makeshift bench in front of him. This fat, robotic millipede of a component would change his life for ever.
He savoured the moment by controlling his impatience and making himself a cup of coffee as his thoughts ran wild. He sat down and pored over his drawings. Then he double checked component values and connections, a task he had repeated many times. Satisfied, once again, that everything was correct, he walked over to his blackboard and worked his way through the complex mathematical equations, pausing only to put a multiplication sign between two consecutive infinity symbols.
Good job I noticed that, he thought, *my future could have been spent as a blob of quivering jelly*.
What these equations told him was that mankind's age old dream of invisibility was, in fact, no longer a

dream – it was a reality.

This erratic pattern of tiny fossilised sea creatures on the blackboard told him that the quadrillions of small particle pairs which came into existence then disappeared each and every second, by supposedly annihilating each other, did no such thing.

His fellow physicists made their observations like a child watching a magician. But he knew different. He knew that these particle pairs were communicating between at least two other dimensions either side of ours. This was the real reason for all the dark matter in the universe. John knew that if he could program his own atomic structure to piggy-back these inter-dimensional particles by using selective, high energy magnetic fields, then his body would allow visible light to pass straight through it without any interference whatsoever. There wouldn't even be a hint of prismatic diffraction. In layman's terms, he would be totally invisible.

He sat in his functional leather office chair and cradled his coffee in both hands, immersing himself deep in thought. Staring blankly over the rim of the mug, he started to speak aloud.

"I'll show them," he said, surprised by the bitterness he heard in his own voice, "they plagiarised my work and won a Nobel Prize. All I wanted was my share of the limelight but they sacked me."

His eyes narrowed.

"I'll show them though. Especially *her*...!"

A tear ran down his cheek as he recalled Sally's last

words as she slammed the front door behind her, "You need help John...you're a fucking nutter!"

Galvanised by the resurfacing of his hurt and indignation, he hurried over to his prototype invisibility machine and plugged in the processor. He adjusted the angle of the huge coiled armatures either side of his body, stood on the aluminium plate at the base of the machine and switched on.

There was no loud noise, flashing lights or electric arcs as in science fiction books and films – he just seemed to blink silently out of existence. The first indication that he still existed was a loud groan and the sound of someone stumbling around the room bumping into the furniture.

"I'm blind!" He screamed as he continued to stumble around.

John now realised the one small fact he'd overlooked. If light was passing unhindered through his body, then no light would be activating the rods and cones of his retinas. Thus he was totally blind. How he wished he hadn't spotted that missing multiplication sign. From where he now stood, the future as a blob of quivering jelly didn't seem so bad after all.

TOM'S BETRAYAL

Sue swallowed hard as she felt the tension rising again. She recognised the now familiar sickly feelings in her stomach along with the throbbing temples. She knew she'd have to tackle him sooner or later, but that didn't stop her dreading the moment.

A trickle of cold sweat ran down her back, further soaking her already damp top. The more she thought about it the more upset she felt.

Sue and Tom had been married for over fifteen years and had never kept secrets from each other. But that had all changed in the last couple of weeks. Things seemed to be very different now. She suddenly realised how much she'd come to rely and depend on Tom during the years of their marriage. The thought of life without Tom filled her with fear and dread. She knew that if the worst happened and he *did* leave, then she'd cope all right - but It would be a very unhappy life for her and the boys, there was no denying that.

"I've *got* to ask him," she muttered aloud to herself.

As she started to prepare the evening meal, she recalled how she overheard the telephone conversation that aroused her suspicions. She had already noticed that Tom was acting a bit strange all week. It was as though he had something on his mind.

Every time she tried to broach the subject he either

changed the subject or avoided it completely and found a little job that needed doing. The final straw came when he offered to take her to the DIY store for some paint and wallpaper. She knew then he was trying to distract her. Something was troubling him and he didn't want to tell her about it.

Then came that phone call.

Sue had gone to empty the kitchen bin into the outside rubbish bin when she heard Tom's voice. He was using his mobile phone in the back garden and she just caught the tail end of the conversation.

"No I haven't told Sue yet," he said, "I'm going to see Sally on Friday, *then* I'll tell her. I'm not looking forward to it but it's got to be done."

When Tom rang home on Friday and told Sue that he'd be working late she braced herself for the worst. He had made a point of never working late on a Friday before. He always said that Friday evening was the start of the weekend, and weekends should be time spent with the family, but this time, the family came second. He didn't get home until well after nine o'clock.

Sue's recollections of the previous week's events were disturbed when she heard Tom coming into the kitchen. Dragging herself back to the present she turned and forced a smile as he entered.

She wiped her hands on her apron, walked over and kissed him.

"Hi Tom, fed up watching TV? Never mind you can give me a hand here ... you can peel a few spuds if you like."

Without answering Tom got the potato peeler from the cutlery drawer and tipped some potatoes into the stainless steel sink.

"No silly joke about cooking being women's work," Sue quipped, "are you OK Tom?"

He didn't reply.

Sue felt slightly alarmed at the silence. She knew all Tom's corny, clichéd jokes off by heart and when he didn't jump at the opportunity to demonstrate his schoolboy humour it was another sign.

She raised her voice.

"Tom, are you all right?"

"Yes I'm fine," Tom said, snapping out of it, "it's just that ... there's something I need to tell you."

As soon as the words left his lips, the back kitchen door burst open and their twelve year old twin sons, Kevin and John, burst in.

"Dad, Mum, we won ... we're in the final," shouted Kevin.

"I scored two," added John.

Tom's resolve melted away.

"I'll tell you later," he said as he disappeared back into the lounge with the excited twins.

Later, as they all sat down for their meal, with the boys still recounting every second of their football match, Tom's thoughts drifted elsewhere. He knew that Sally would still be waiting and wondering what was happening.

He couldn't leave her alone much longer. He'd have

to tell Sue ... and soon. He looked at her across the table. She was smiling warmly at the twins as they went on and on about their game and the forthcoming final. Her good looks *still* took his breath away after all these years. With her long blond hair and slim figure, she was still as beautiful as she was on the day he married her. He hoped that when he told her about Sally that she'd hold it together and not think too badly of him for betraying her.

After the meal Sue stood up and started to collect the dishes. Tom took her hand in his.

"Can you leave those for a moment please Sue?" he asked nervously, "there's something I need to tell you."

She couldn't hide her apprehension as Tom took her hand in his and led her out of the back kitchen door. The silence was broken only by the crunching of the gravel on the pathway as he led her to the tool shed at the bottom end of the garden. She watched him take a deep breath as he opened the door.

"Meet Sally," he said.

Sally rushed out and jumped up putting her mucky paws all over Sue's dress, her long Spaniel tail wagging furiously.

"I Know you're not keen on dogs," Tom protested, "but it was either ours or the dog's home."

"She's gorgeous," Sue interrupted, "anyway, she'll give the boys something to think about other than *football, football, football.*"

Sue laughed with a mixture of happiness and relief as

Tom wrapped his arms around her and kissed her "You make my whole life worthwhile Sue," he said, "I love you so much."

IT SOUNDED LIKE AN EXPLOSION

It sounded like an explosion. It was much more violent than the previous one a couple of minutes earlier. This one was more like a minor earthquake.

I try to move away but there's nowhere I can go. I'm perched on the very edge and in grave danger of falling off. The last thing I need at my age is a head injury! I turn around to see if I can improve my situation.

As usual, she's spread out and has taken most of my side of the bed as well as her own. I try to push her back into her own half without disturbing the quilt and releasing the gas that usually accompanies her nocturnal rumblings. A swift, reflexive elbow into my ribs tells me I'm wasting my time.

I lay in the dark alone with my thoughts. I plighted my troth to this beached whale fifty-two years ago and I still love her as much as I did on the night we met, warts, farts and all.

My mind drifts back.

I'd not long been discharged from my national service and had been serving in Egypt during the Suez Crisis. My friends had surprised me with a Saturday night homecoming party at the Caradoc Hotel. I remember it clearly, it was 15th November 1957. I walked into the pub to the strains of The Crickets singing *That'll be the Day*, which was the number one hit record at the time.

My mates grabbed me immediately and pulled me into the back room. There were many small, cosy rooms in the pubs those days, rather than the large lounges which seem to be the main feature of today's pubs. Our room had a roaring coal fire with a big iron fireplace. There were bell pushes at the back of the seats to ring for service. Those were the days eh!

I was pushed into a corner seat and had a Threlly's brown mixed and a double rum plonked in front of me. I wondered if I'd last the night.

Shortly after, a tall, slim blond girl came in. She was gorgeous! Our eyes locked and my life changed forever. For the next two years our love grew and our lives entwined so tightly that we might have been one person.

It wasn't until after the wedding I found out she was capable of farting. I was traumatised the first time I heard her. The sudden, rip-snorting sound was bad enough, but how could my Goddess produce such foul smelling stenches? There was no hint of this in the marriage vows. Nor was there mention of the nightly invasion and annexation of my bed space. Had Adolph Hitler been so subtle, he might have united Europe long before the Common Market.

When I recovered from the fact that my princess was just another human being, we settled down to the serious grind that is married life and produced three wonderful children who are now carrying our family torch into a distant future that we will never see.

The distraction embedded in everyday life stole away

one of our most precious gifts, the gift of time. Like most other people of our age we bemoan its passing and wonder where it's all gone. We may find the answer soon, but I'm in no particular hurry.

Feeling sleepy again, I smile, turn towards her and kiss her bare shoulder. She purrs sleepily. I put my arm around her and cup her warm breast. She shudders with pleasure.

I still have it ... so does she!

HARVEST TIME

Professor John Cumine turned up the collar of his padded overcoat. The New Mexico late summer nights were surprisingly cold. He wondered whether his shivering was due solely to the cold breeze, or was it helped by fear of the alien spacecraft, one of which had landed a mere two hundred metres away.
Why Roswell? he thought.
He remembered the stories his grandfather had told him about the space ship that crashed way back in 1947. A *flying Saucer* his grandfather had called it. Nobody seemed to know what really happened. The event was steeped in so much mystery and secrecy that John became fixated with space travel and all things astronomical. This led to him becoming one of the most eminent scientists at NASA. At forty-two years old, he was the man everyone turned to when there were problems to be solved.
The alien space ships had been in stationary orbit for eight days and seemed to hover motionless in the sky for as far as the horizon in every direction. They were so evenly spaced, it was as though Earth was encased in a huge crystal lattice. There was no warning of their arrival; they just seemed to blink into existence. Mankind was in a state of flux, wondering whether or not the beings in charge of the ships were friendly and peaceful.
It was eventually agreed that the United Nations

would send an ambassador to try and establish the purpose for the alien's visit to Earth. The man chosen for the task was none other than Professor John Cumine. His background in space exploration, and the fact that he was a leading member of the NASA Mediation Council, made him the ideal candidate for the task.

John and his fellow scientists made various attempts to communicate with the ship's occupants, including coded pulsed light beams and radio transmission of mathematical formulae. All failed. It was now a matter of waiting for the visitors to make the first move.

On the eve of the eighth day, one of the spacecraft sited above Roswell started to descend. It landed in a farmer's field on the outskirts of the town. John, along with some top brass from the New Mexico Military Institute, was flown in by helicopter to the site of the active spacecraft. The world held its breath.

As he waited, John thought back to the argument he'd had with his wife, Nina, and their two teenage daughters when he agreed to take on the role of ambassador.

"Why *you*? Why is it always *you*? Haven't you done *enough* for them?" his wife Nina had screamed through her tears, "isn't it time you thought of me and the girls for a change?"

She slapped him hard across the face and then wrapped her arms tightly about him, pushing her face into his chest muting her sobs. Their daughters, Susan and Maria, also crying, sat on the settee with handkerchiefs to their faces. Nina gave it one last try "Don't do it John, *please*, don't do it."

"I have no choice now," he said, "there's no time to brief anybody else. Anyway, we're probably worrying about nothing. I'll be back before you know it."

He tore himself away from her, picked up his suitcase, and climbed aboard the jeep for his trip to the airfield. His eyes filled as Nina's cries faded into the distance as he was driven away from their home.

The sound of machinery being operated snapped John out of his reflective sadness.

The floodlights placed around the site were switched on, bringing what seemed to be instant daylight. He dabbed his eyes with the back of his hands and looked up just in time to see a ramp descending from the underside of the ship. The time had come. He got into the waiting jeep and was driven almost to the base of the ramp. Swallowing his regrets at agreeing to become mankind's representative, he made his way slowly up the ramp and into the cavernous opening of the ship.

Some hallway, he thought.

His heart raced as he was met by two of the ship's strange, reptilian like, occupants.

They picked him up by his arms and legs and half carried, half dragged him unceremoniously along one of the corridors that led off from the entrance chamber. They eventually passed through another opening and, without concern, they dropped him to the floor, totally oblivious to the pain and discomfort it caused him.

Shocked, he gathered his senses and looked around, conscious of a foul smell emanating from his wrists where the aliens had held him. As he stood up, he heard a hissing, raucous voice addressing him.

"What is your name?"

He turned to see another reptilian being, identical to the two that had carried him from the ship's entrance. It was brown and scaly, about eight feet tall and powerfully built. Its arms and legs seemed to move without joints and were continuously flexible. On top of a squat neck was a large froglike head with powerfully built jaws and a row of protruding fangs.

"I said, what is your name?" the alien repeated.

"John ... John Cumine," he stuttered, "thank you for seeing me."

"Tell me why you came aboard our vessel."

"I've been elected to come and see you; to find out the purpose of your visit."

"You are wasting your time."

"I've also been asked to find out how long you are staying on Earth."

"We will stay until we have feasted on the entire Human Race and most of the higher warm-blooded life forms."

John was stunned into silence. Fear gripped his entire being. Finally he spoke, but his words rang hollow in his own head.

"Just like that? You invade our planet and without any effort to communicate with us, you decide to *kill* us all?"

"The fact that you killed the occupants of our reconnaissance craft in nineteen forty seven did not seem to cause *your* species much concern."

John tried again to reason with the large reptile.

"Doesn't it bother you how much pain and suffering you'll cause?"

"If we do not eat, we die. I am sure you understand this. After all, your own species breed animals and eat them when they are in prime condition."

"Yes, but they don't suffer. We kill them humanely. We don't cause them pain."

"We are completely without empathy. Apart from fear, your feelings are of no consequence to us."

"Fear? Why is fear so important?"

"When you are afraid, certain chemicals are released in your brain, these chemicals have a great effect on how your flesh tastes. That is why we will eat you alive. There are, in fact, many reptilian life forms on your own planet which do not eat unless their prey is alive, so you must have some understanding of this.

Some of your own species like to eat meat from animals which have their blood continuously leaked from their body in order to lighten their flesh.

That is not so much different from our taste. You also display behaviour that we cannot understand, you hunt and kill your fellow animals for pleasures unconnected with feeding yourselves. These are, by your own definition, cruel deeds. What do you say in answer to this?"

"It seems I've been wasting my time. I'll go and tell the council of your decision."

"You will go nowhere, nor will you tell your fellow earth dwellers anything."

"What do you mean?"

"I mean you are about to be eaten. Our ancestors seeded this planet with its many life forms millions of years ago. It is time for us to reap the harvest."

The alien leapt across the room in one bound and took hold of John by wrapping its long fingers around his neck. It started to squeeze as John struggled to talk.

"Let go of me, I came here in good faith."

Ignoring him totally, the alien sunk its teeth deep into John's shoulder and pushed a spiked piece of equipment into his chest. John's screams were ignored. He started to feel dizzy and weak and slumped to the floor, immobile, but fully conscious. The alien looked down into his face and spoke.

"That bite has paralysed you, and that gauge I pushed into your chest will tell me how your fear is affecting your blood. I will eat you a little at a time to instil as much fear as possible. Our saliva contains a very strong coagulant so you can rule out the luxury of bleeding to death.

Your wife and children are on their way here as I speak. It always heightens the fear factor when families with young offspring are eaten within sight of each other. With the use of our advanced technology, your family will be kept alive for many days. You may wonder why I am telling you this, well, to put it quite simply, the more I scare you the better you will taste. In fact the gauge I have just inserted indicates it may be worth sampling you already. Just a few fingers perhaps, you will not be using them again."

John watches helplessly as the alien lifts his arm and bites into his right hand. The searing pain and the sound of splintering bone sicken him. Beneath his screams he reflects on the pain to come for him, his family, and the whole human race. Intense fear causes his blood chemistry to change even more, this results a groan of pleasure from the alien.

"Hmm, just one more bite." It slavers.

John's screams, and the sound of crunching bone, echo around the metal walls of the chamber ...

SPINNING ENID

One Monday morning in January, as Noddy was driving along in his little car, he noticed a bus shelter where a large queue of people were waiting. As he passed he heard a man's voice calling out his name.
'Noddy, Noddy,' he shouted.
He pulled over, stopped his car, and turned to see who was calling him. It was Big Ears. He was standing by the bus stop.
'Hello Big Ears,' he shouted back, 'were you calling me?'
'Yes,' Big Ears replied, 'any chance of giving me a lift?'
'Of course I'll give you a lift,' chuckled Noddy, 'you know how much I like helping people, get in.'
As Big Ears clambered eagerly into the passenger seat and made himself comfortable, Noddy glowed with pride and satisfaction. He *really did* love helping people.
'What are you doing in London anyway?' Noddy continued.
'I'm just off to Harrods,' replied Big Ears, 'there's a sale on and I've heard they're selling some stuff off at half price.'
'Half price eh,' cooed Noddy, 'that's nearly fifty per cent.'
'It *is* fifty per cent,' chided Big Ears, 'now can we get a move on? I don't want to miss all the bargains.'

Noddy pressed the button to start his little car – but *nothing* happened. Not a sausage.

'Oh dear,' Noddy groaned, 'it's broken down again.'

'*Again?*' said Big Ears impatiently. 'You mean it's *always* breaking down?'

'Yes, I'm afraid it is,' replied Noddy sadly, 'five or six times a day now!'

'Then what's the point of offering people lifts?' barked Big Ears.

'Well, if you remember,' Noddy said correcting him, 'I didn't offer you a lift, you asked me could I *give* you a lift. Nobody in their right mind would offer people lifts in a car like this, would they now?'

Big Ears was speechless. He looked back at the bus stop and noticed that all the people were gone. He imagined the whole busload getting off at Harrods and picking up all the bargains. He'd missed his bus and they only came every two hours. He was stuck with Noddy and there was no getting out of it. The idea of getting a cab made him shudder. The thought of handing all that money over to a cab driver made him feel nauseous. In the meantime, Noddy had been rummaging in the car boot until he eventually found his starting handle. He came alongside the passenger door and offered it to Big Ears.

'Take this and turn the engine over while I hold the start button,' he said imperiously.

'A starting handle?' asked Big Ears in astonishment, 'Who on earth has a starting handle these days?'

'I do,' replied Noddy, his patience wearing thin,

'Now do you want to get to this sale or not?'

'I know,' said Big Ears as he smiled weakly at Noddy, 'why don't *I* hold the start button and *you* turn the starting handle?

'Because I'm the only one insured to drive this car. It's a Noddy car for God's sake. You can't have Big Ears driving a Noddy car. What would people say?'

Big Ears reluctantly held out his hand, took the oily starting handle from Noddy and went around to the front of the car. He put it in the hole in the bumper and started turning it with a limp-wristed action.

'Not like that,' Noddy screamed, 'if it kicks back it'll take your fucking hand off!'

Noddy showed him the correct way to use the starting handle and between them they eventually got the car going. He gave Big Ears an old piece of rag to wipe his hands and soon they were on their way again.

'How come you didn't use your own car anyway?' Noddy asked casually.

'You're joking aren't you?' said Big Ears rhetorically. 'With the cost of petrol these days, and the London surcharge, it's hardly worth owning a car.'

But you don't mind getting a lift in mine, at my expense, you tight bastard, Noddy thought grudgingly.

Not for the first time in his life he cursed his desire to help others.

Why was I born with this compulsion to help others all the time? It must be great to not give a shit and just ignore those who need help - to be free to enjoy your own life and not worry about every Sad Sack you happen to bump into.

'Nearly there,' Noddy said as he was about to turn into Brompton road, but as he spoke, there was a loud spluttering noise from the car's engine and it shuddered to a halt. Once again Big Ears was crawling around on his hands and knees turning the uncooperative starting handle while Noddy pushed the starting button. By the time they gave up, Big Ears was drenched in sweat. His face was black with oil from the hands that wiped his brow. As he stood there catching his breath, he saw Noddy jump out of the car and go to the boot.

'I've just remembered,' he said in a eureka tone, 'it might be out of petrol.'

He took a petrol container and a funnel from the boot, took the petrol cap off and poured the contents of the can into the tank. The hollow sound from the tank confirmed what he already knew - it was empty. Once back in their seats, the car started first time, and much to Big Ears relief, without the need for the starting handle.

The remainder of the journey was carried out in silence but the atmosphere could have been cut with a knife. As they pulled up alongside Harrods, their attention was drawn to a large notice in the window. It read:

'Due to the huge success of our end of season sale, the discounted prices have finished earlier than expected. Normal business is resumed.'

Big Ears read the notice and jumped angrily out of Noddy's little car, slamming the door.

'Why don't you buy a *new* car ... after all you must have made a tidy packet from all those *1970s hit records.*'

'A drop in the ocean compared to your income from *The Duchy*, you ungrateful pig," replied Noddy as he clenched his fists in anger.

BUS STOP

Well, here it is, the bus stop. The 61 bus stop to be precise. Nothing much has changed really, I mean everything's still in the same place. The three banks at the island, they're not banks any more mind you and they've been many things since they closed down. There was Barclay's on the corner of Linacre Road and Knowsley Road, National Westminster on the corner of Stanley Road and Linacre Lane, and the TSB on the corner of Linacre Lane and Linacre Road. I opened my first bank account at the TSB in 1965. I was eighteen then and I still remember how important I felt when I got my first cheque book with my name printed on the cheques.

The North Park doesn't look as though it's changed at all from here, and the Linacre pub half way up the canal bridge still looks the same. My old paper shop opposite has closed down though. I got my Daily Mirror and 10 Woodbines there every weekday for over 15 years.

This bus stop is where I first met Brenda. I lived in Sonning Avenue, Ford, and I worked at the Mother's Pride bakery in Stopgate Lane, so I used to get the 55 to the North Park and then get the 61 from this stop to work.

This was my routine each day from when I left school in July 1962. We didn't hang around in those days and within a week I had started my working life.

I coasted along for 10 months or so then, Wham! On Monday 6th of May 1963, there she was – a new girl had arrived at the bus stop – She was beauty personified. What you have to remember is that not many working class people had cars in those days, so you got the same people queuing at the same bus stop each day, and when someone new came along they stood out. Within a few days I had overcome my shyness and asked her name, it was Brenda. She told me that she lived in Elm Road, Seaforth and caught the number 16 bus to the North Park. She worked in Vernons Pools and got the same 61 bus as I did, although she got off a couple of stops later.

Going to work became a joy. I couldn't wait to get to the 61 bus stop every day and see her. Before long we were seeing each other every night. Although it was possible for me to walk to her parent's house in Elm Road in 15 to 20 minutes, we always agreed to meet at our bus stop where we'd spend the night kissing and cuddling – much to the disdain of others waiting for their bus. When the time came for us to fully consummate our relationship there was only one place to be considered. With first time nerves and the fear of being discovered, that was, indeed, a night to remember.

As was the pattern in the early 60s, we had a short engagement and an inexpensive wedding, followed by a weekend in Blackpool, after which we moved in with her Mum and Dad. Those were the days eh!

Following the birth of our son, Michael, Brenda had

to give up her job to look after him.

In the meantime, I had to grab all the overtime going as we tried hard to save up for a mortgage deposit. A two up two down terraced house with an outside toilet could be bought for around £750 – around about a year's wages for most people.

The long hours I was working and the cramped conditions we were living in eventually started to take their toll. I hated the long hours and Brenda hated me leaving her on her own to cope with the baby – that's when the constant bickering started and we began to get on each other's nerves.

Some mornings, while waiting for the 61, I would take great pleasure in booting the corrugated iron of our bus shelter with my steel toe capped boots. Its dull clanging as I imagined it feeling pain was therapeutic music to my ears. This bus shelter had a lot to answer for.

Shortly after Michael's second birthday Brenda got a letter from one of the girls in Vernon's Pools. She was invited to a reunion of former employees at the Crown Hotel in Norris Green the following Saturday. I agreed to stay home with Michael so that Brenda could relax and enjoy herself without needing to worry about a babysitter. Saturday evening dragged on as I sat watching both Michael and the clock on the mantelpiece. I knew that at 11.35pm, Brenda would catch the 61 bus from the Crown Hotel.

This would give her plenty of time to catch the last 16 which didn't leave the Pier Head until 12 midnight.

It was then I thought I'd surprise her.

If I got to our bus stop by 11.50, I could greet her as she got off the 61. Perhaps we could have a kiss and a cuddle for old time's sake. Her mum agreed to watch Michael for the following hour or so and I went to meet Brenda.

By the time I got to the North Park I realised that I was in plenty of time. I strolled around the corner into Linacre Lane. I smiled as I saw a courting couple in our bus stop. They were practically eating each other alive. His hands were everywhere and she was loving every minute of it. It reminded me of mine and Brenda's early passion for each other. My smile spread to a grin as I remembered how Brenda and me used to hate other people coming into the bus stop while we were so engrossed.

Feeling generous, I decided to stand some distance away from the bus stop and wait for Brenda's 61. This way I wouldn't disturb the young lovers. I couldn't help but overhear the couple in the bus stop as things heated up to the point where they were actually having sex.

Feeling a bit embarrassed, I moved further away until things cooled down and they started whispering to each other. Before long, Brenda's bus came into view and I crossed over to the stop opposite our special stop. It was a bit of a shock when the bus didn't even stop.

It went straight past the bus stop and round the island into Knowsley Road. I was still trying to figure out what had happened when the couple came out of our bus stop.

"Don't go yet." he said as she broke away from him.

"I have to," she replied, "that's the bus I was supposed to have been on."

I recognised the voice instantly. It was Brenda.

She told me later that she'd caught an earlier bus so that she could spend some time with this man who had turned up to the reunion. Apparently, she'd had a crush on him before I met her.

I moved back in with my parents the following day. That was February 1967 and I've lived there ever since. I inherited the house when mum and dad passed on.

Why then, am I standing here at our ill-fated bus stop and reliving old, unpleasant memories from the past? You might well ask, after all, it's 2012 now and those memories no longer bother me. The point is, I still need to catch the 61 bus, but now I get off at Aigbuth Vale.

Mine and Sarah's special bus stop.

SERMON

As I sat down to my breakfast this morning – a boiled egg and a piece of toast – I noticed that my housekeeper, Mrs Smith, had placed my egg upside down in the eggcup. I can only assume that she was distracted by the fact that a murder had taken place in the street outside just hours earlier.

I make this assumption because she's known for many years that I'm a passionate Big-endian, and has never made such a gross error before.

As I cracked the top of the egg with my spoon, I reflected on how Mr Jones's skull had splintered as a gang of eight hooded thugs had stamped on his head in an effort to steal his car. Mr Jones had defended his car with his life because it was his only means of getting to work, and making his nightly visits to be with his wife at the local Hospice.

Now it is my duty, as a minister of the church, to stand before you and reiterate the weekly messages of Love, Faith, Hope and charity. But before I can do this I need to reconcile that which I teach with that which I truly believe. Unfortunately, I find myself in a position where I can no longer do this. In the shadow of this growing army of disenfranchised sub-human thugs, my formerly honest and heartfelt words now ring hollow.

These social misfits destroy the quality of life with impunity.

They laugh at the impotence of the law and totally devalue all that is good in the world. They stunt the development of well behaved and caring youngsters who just happen to live in the same area. These marauding young thugs present a bigger and more viable threat to our country and our way of life than Adolph Hitler ever did.

It is with this in mind that I will be resigning my post as parish priest at St James' later this week. Consequently, this will be my last sermon, but before I go, let me say this: In the future I will be taking on another, more practical and useful role in society. I will be heading the local, newly formed vigilante group. When we encounter a gang of hooded thugs bullying and intimidating people, we will storm in with baseball bats and mete out the real, on the spot justice they deserve and understand.

Machine guns would be much more efficient of course, but there's nothing quite as satisfying as the clunk of solid wood on the thick, uncaring adolescent bone of an evil thug.

God bless you all...Now where's my balaclava...?

STAG NIGHT

Debbie kissed the kids, Deborah and Joseph, goodnight.
"Be good for your dad," she said. Then made her way down the hallway as she called out to them, "and bed at nine o'clock, don't forget."
"OK mummy," they called after her in unison.
They were well used to this nightly ritual.
She sighed as she stopped at the front door with Joe who had accompanied her.
"What's up?" Joe asked, "don't you feel up to it tonight?"
"I don't feel up to it any night lately," Debbie replied, "but the money's good, and with the wedding coming up we need it!"
Joe nodded in agreement. Debbie was right. Her part-time evening work as a Social Worker paid almost as much as his fork lift driving job at the cement factory. Debbie, 32, and Joe, 36, had been happily living together for over eight years. They met at a nightclub in Blackpool and were immediately attracted to each other. After catching each other's eye all night, Joe could no longer resist her long blond hair, warm blue eyes and gorgeous figure so he finally plucked up the courage to speak to her. It turned out that they had both been married and divorced early on in their lives. They had so much in common that within hours of meeting they were smitten.

Nine months after meeting they bought a three bedroom semi together.

Now, seven and a half years later, they were raising their two children Deborah, 5, and Joseph, 4. Although Debbie and Joe both knew that they loved each other and would be together forever, there was always that little bit of fear in the back of their minds. Because of their earlier mistakes, neither of them felt prepared to commit to another marriage.

At least that was how it was until Debbie decided the wedding was long overdue.

"Are you sure?" Joe said when she brought the subject up. "After all," he continued, "we've both tried it before with disastrous results."

"That was then," Debbie replied, "we were both far too young to realise what we were doing. Do you think you'll ever leave me and the kids?" she went on.

"Of course not," he said, "how can you even ask such a question?"

Debbie smiled at his reaction. The look on Joe's face told her what she already knew, that he loved her and the kids more than life itself.

"So by having the kids, we've already made the biggest commitment that any couple can make to each other. Wouldn't you agree?"

Joe smiled. "You're right as usual. It's time to put the past where it belongs ... in the past. The day we get married I'll be the happiest man in the world."

After that conversation their lives stepped up a gear,

both working, looking after the kids, and now a wedding to arrange. There never seemed to be enough hours in the day.

As Joe prepared for his stag night, Debbie got the kids ready and packed their clothes for the wedding the following day. She, Deborah, and Joseph would be staying at her mum and dad's house so she could prepare without Joe seeing her wedding dress. As Debbie said goodnight to Joe, she reflected on how his looks had improved with age. His tall frame had filled out beautifully and with his dark eyes and black curly hair he could have been a male model. She gave him the usual parting advice. "Don't forget your key, don't have too much to drink, have you got your phone?" And a couple of new ones he hadn't heard before, "don't let your mates tie you to a lamp post or anything silly like that ... and no strippers!"

Joe dropped Debbie and the kids off at her mum and dad's house in a taxi then headed off into the Golden Eagle pub in the town centre to meet his mates. As the evening progressed, Joe felt increasing unease as his friends kept grinning at him for no apparent reason.

They've got something planned, he thought to himself. He was right. On the stroke of ten o'clock, a woman came into the pub lounge carrying a ghetto blaster which she placed on a table near Joe and switched it on. Loud dance music filled the room.

One of Joe's mates jumped to his feet and shouted at the top of his voice,

"Gentlemen, let me introduce The Horned Temptress."

All the others laughed heartily as Joe stared at her in disbelief.

She was wearing shiny black PVC pants, which showed off her perfectly curved figure to the full, fish-net stockings and six inch heels.

Her bra was also black PVC, as was the horned mask which totally covered her face.

She danced in front of Joe for a while then sat astride him and unbuttoned his shirt before pouring oil onto her hands and massaged it into his chest. By the time the music finished, Joe was totally bare-chested and feeling guilty about how much he fancied her.

If Debbie ever finds out about this she'll kill me, he thought.

Next day, the wedding went very well. Debbie was the beautiful bride everyone predicted she'd be and the children looked so cute in their outfits. The flowers were beautiful and the service went like clockwork. When it came to exchanging vows though, Debbie noticed that Joe wasn't quite himself. He seemed a bit hesitant, as though he had something on his mind.

Debbie smiled at him. She knew she'd make him feel better. She had spent many years relaxing people and making them feel at ease. After all, it was part of her job as *The Horned Temptress.*

THE CRASH

Pablo Rodrigues guided his animals through the South American dustbowl he called his farm. Pablo was a proud man and was deservedly well respected by his fellow tribesmen. His father had died penniless when Pablo was a small boy and his mother had to rely on the generosity of the tribe to rear Pablo and his brothers and sisters.
I am going to provide a good life for myself and my family when I grow up, Pablo had promised himself.
And indeed he had, with three cows, six goats and two dozen hens, Pablo was, in local terms, a very rich man. At least he was, until the day of the helicopter.
The helicopter landed not far from Pablo's adobe hut and a strangely attired man got out carrying with him some pieces of paper. He greeted Pablo with a row of grinning white teeth which reminded him of an angry monkey. Pablo hoped that this strange man would not try to bite him. His fears were allayed when the man tried to explain to Pablo about the world recession and how everyone was now less wealthy than they had been a year ago. Pablo's grasp of English was nothing spectacular, but it was enough for him to get by and had served him well in the market place for more than twenty years. He knew the strange man had got it wrong.
"You have made a mistake, senõr," Pablo asserted, "Last year I had three cows, six goats and twenty-

four hens and this year I still have three cows, six goats and twenty-four hens. So you see, senõr, I am still a wealthy man. Look at my wife and children; look how plump they are. Do they look hungry to you?"

The strange man shook his head and tutted.

"That's got nothing to do with it," he said, "look, let me show you."

He unrolled the bundle of papers he was carrying and laid them out so they could both see them clearly. Pablo looked down at the multi-coloured pie charts and rows of figures, most of them underlined in red.

"They are very pretty senõr, they would look very nice hanging on the wall of your home. What will you do with them?"

"What will I do with them?" replied the strange man, "I'm a Chartered accountant. This is what I do. These are bread and butter to me!"

"You will eat them senõr?" Pablo asked in astonishment, "they do not look very tasty?"

"Of course I won't eat them!" roared the man getting more impatient by the second. "They tell me how much everything is worth. Look at your hut. How much do you think it you could get for it now because of the recession?"

"It is not for sale senõr."

"I'm not trying to buy it man. I'm just trying to establish any loss of value since the start of the recession."

"Will this recession make the rain come through my roof? Will it take away the happy memories of my children's laughter as they grew strong in the comfort of my home? I think not senõr. My house is worth what it has always been worth and no pretty coloured pieces of paper will ever change that."

The strange man took one of his blood pressure pills and started to babble incoherently as he staggered back towards the helicopter.

That evening, as Pablo and his family sat replete enjoying the warm glow from their fire, they talked about what the strange man with the grinning monkey's teeth had said.

Their communal laughter echoed happily around the small dusty farm.

THE DECISION

Sabrina had always scorned his lack of ability to make decisions, but this time Alec was going to prove her wrong. He now knew that true power lay in the ability to act quickly and decisively under pressure, and in any given situation. Sabrina could do that with ease, which was why she had controlled his life for so long. It was as though she was living two lives simultaneously and he was just a passenger in one of them. What surprised him most though was that he had not realised this before. She had steered him blindly through forty-five years of marriage like a bull with a ring through its nose; beating his malleable soul to a compliant pulp in the process. It was only when he came upon a certain book at the local car boot sale that he began to understand.
He stood looking fixatedly at the pasting table-cum-stall. There it lay, tilted at a rakish angle, showing off to the bric-a-brac that surrounded it. Its title screamed at Alec and goaded him to buy it.
'HOW TO OVERCOME INDECISIVENESS,' it said, *'buy me if you dare!'*
It was as though the book knew that Sabrina had banned him from acquiring any more books. Alec, being an avid reader, was familiar with all subjects and genres, but there was something about this particular book he could not resist.
He took a shifty glance to his left and saw that

Sabrina was three stalls behind, looking through some cushion covers.

"How much is that book?" he whispered pointing it out to the stallholder.

"Fifty pence," the man replied.

Alec pinched his lower lip and shuffled from foot to foot while trying to make up his mind, wondering if he dare ask Sabrina for fifty pence. He puffed out his cheeks and continued to dither for a further minute or so. At this point, the stallholder grabbed the book and thrust it into Alec's hands.

"Here mate," he said, "take it, have it for nowt. It looks like you desperately need it."

Alec whispered his thanks, put the book under his jacket and scurried back to Sabrina.

When they arrived home, Alec made Sabrina and himself a cup of tea, settled her in her comfortable armchair, and gave her a plate of her favourite ginger snap biscuits. Following this, he set off upstairs to one of the spare bedrooms.

Now that the children had left home, this particular bedroom was just used for storage. At the back of the room was a large double wardrobe with a space behind it just large enough for a small man to snuggle into. This was where Alec did most of his reading. He had kitted it out with a couple of fluffy pillows and a duvet. It was here he could curl up with a book and hide from the world until Sabrina's hollow, bellowing voice summoned him.

Alec settled himself down on the floor at the back of

the wardrobe with his new book, his cup of tea, and his small plate of ginger snaps. He stared at the biscuits and crumpled his face into a scowl.

Why couldn't we have custard creams for a change? he thought.

He thought back to the one-sided argument he'd had with Sabrina when she sent him for their weekly shop and he dared to buy custard creams instead of ginger snaps. She totally embarrassed him by raging at him to take them back and replace them with ginger snaps. He would have hidden them and just bought a packet of ginger snaps, but she didn't allow him to have any money of his own. Not a penny. It was another way of controlling him.

He switched on his makeshift lamp. From this cosy little space he had travelled all over the world, journeyed into space fighting intergalactic wars and made love to the most beautiful women in history - all with the help of the world's greatest literature.

He resentfully bit into one of his ginger snap biscuits, opened his new book and read the inside cover:

'Decision making is an important part of one's life. It helps us to take control, accept responsibility, achieve success and happiness, and find out who we really are.

Indecisiveness, though, complicates all aspects of our lives. It results in abdication from making decisions, it stunts growth and development. It also evokes feelings of powerlessness, inadequacy, frustration, envy and cynicism.' it said.

Alec allowed these words to filter into his brain. He

read them over and over again. Eventually he was so moved, he spoke aloud.

"This is it," he asserted, "this is the book I've been waiting for. This book is going to change my life, I can feel it."

It was a true epiphany. The light shone as brightly as it had done for Saul on the road to Damascus. The difference being that Alec did not go blind. Instead, he suddenly became aware of what had been happening to him over the years.

"Things are *definitely* going to change," he confirmed aloud.

Two weeks later, Alec sat in his bolthole drinking a hot mug of tea and munching from a large plate of custard creams. Steeped in one of his more racy books, he shuddered with pleasure as he turned the page to the last chapter.

He was happy now, happier than he had ever been in the last forty-five years of his marriage. He had finally put Sabrina in her place. It wasn't easy as she tried to browbeat him into submission, but the book gave him strength. For once he'd made a decision and asserted himself. He wondered if Sabrina had been proud of him in some, small way.

If only I'd had the guts to do it years ago, he thought.

He looked up at the ceiling. The large patch that had leaked through from the attic above was changing colour again. First it had been crimson, then light brown, then dark brown, and now it was going black. Alec purred with satisfaction and returned to his book. "Life is Good!" he said aloud.

THE HOUSEWIFE

Tom Strutter plucked at his nasal hair with a small pair of tweezers and smiled at his magnified reflection in the small, circular shaving mirror on his desk.

"Well done old chap," he said aloud, "very well done indeed!"

His sales team had just closed another deal that would make his fellow directors sit up and take notice.

If I could convert this month's Good Boy points into Green Shield Stamps, he gloated to himself, *I'd have enough to get a brand new BMW.*

Tom was a real high flyer. He ruled his sales department with an iron fist and took no prisoners. The men under him trembled at the mere mention of his name. His ruthless, although highly successful, sales performance strategy was to sack one of his sales team every six months. The sales figures would be added up and the person who came last would say goodbye to his company car keys, pick up his personal belongings, and walk through the majestic gates of World Wide Widgets for the very last time.

Buzzing with pride, Tom decided it was time to reward himself, the ritual sacking could wait.

He locked his office door, sat down and Googled his favourite site,

Very Naughty Housewives of the UK.

His whole body trembled with delight as he clicked on the New Posts tab. As the page loaded up he considered his ambivalent feelings for these nude and scantily clad women. They both disgusted and excited him at the same time. These housewives were by no means glamour models, some were in fact downright ugly, but he was so driven by his compulsion that he had actually met up with some of them in hotel rooms and purged his shameful desires. The new posts loaded as a slide show and he clicked through them eagerly, drooling and slobbering onto his computer keyboard.

Picture fourteen stopped him dead in his tracks. She was a dark haired, Rubenesque woman, about forty years of age. She had a warm smile and very nice eyes. Her well proportioned breasts did her credit, as did her knickers, suspenders and black stockings. The thing that struck him most though was the fact that she was his wife.

He read the accompanying message:

'I'm looking for some fun and excitement in life. Hubby not doing his job in the bedroom department very well. Too busy with other things to give me what I need.'

Tom's face went purple and he logged off. He picked up the phone and angrily stabbed at the buttons.
"Have you done the latest figures?" he raged.
"Send the guy who did the least up here. **Now**!"

A few minutes later, Ian Jones knocked on Tom's door and entered.

"Don't bother with the screaming bit boss," he said, "I've already packed my stuff. I was leaving anyway."

Tom's intended words of rage got wedged in his throat.

"Oh, by the way," Ian continued, "do you want to know why my figures were so low? A couple of months ago I came into your office to see you but you weren't here. Your computer was on so I got a bit curious and checked out your browsing history."

Tom writhed uneasily in his seat and loosened his tie as he felt himself flushing with embarrassment.

"I messaged a lovely woman on that site you like so much, and we're going away together to start a new life. Apparently her old man's a sales director and he's too busy with other things to give her what she needs in the bedroom department.

She needn't worry though, I'll soon make up for that."

THE GLOWING EMBERS OF LOVE

Waiting for her bus, Mary couldn't wait to get home. "Fancy getting a job at my age," she thought. "George will be so proud of me."
It was sixty years since she and George married, and yet to her, it only seemed like yesterday that they were standing nervously in front of the vicar reciting their marriage vows. She remembered how difficult it was to stop herself giggling.
They were childhood sweethearts since they met at her eleventh birthday party, George was the only boy who brought her a present. He blushed bright red as the other boys mocked and teased him, but when she opened the strange-shaped parcel and saw a whip and top - one of the good ones with leather instead of string - she knew there and then that he was the person she wanted to spend the rest of her life with.
From that moment on they were inseparable and counted the days until they were both sixteen and eligible to tie the knot.
The squeal of brakes reached out and dragged her uncomfortably back to the present as her bus pulled up at the stop. She battled, jostled and elbowed her way onto the bus as only senior citizens can. At seventy-six years of age she had gained lots of experience and could mix it with the best of them.
As she settled in her seat, Mary's mind once again drifted back over the years.

She remembered how George always frowned on the idea of her going out to work, but things were so much different now.

He could no longer work, and with the old age pension money buying less and less each week she had no choice.

Anyway, she thought. *It's me who makes the decisions now.*

Although she was sure that George would be proud of her, it would be hard luck on him if he wasn't.

She checked her pocket for reassurance that the fruit of her first week's labour was still there. Mary no longer carried valuables in her handbag. In this day and age a handbag was just a decoy for the muggers. *What a difference this will make.* She thought. *Ninety pounds for five afternoons, that's more than ten times what George earned when we were first married.*

Mary wouldn't say this to him of course. The last thing she wanted in the world was to say anything to hurt his feelings. She remembered how he had always sheltered her from the world's cruel ways - and for this she would always be grateful - but it was her turn now and she was determined to look after George for as long as she lived.

She started every day by telling him how much she loved him, just as he did to her for as long as he was able.

"You've got to be old to know real love," Mary said under her breath. "It's a bit like a coal fire ... when all the flames of passion have gone out and you're left with that nice warm, comfortable glow ... That's what *real* love's like."

The bus slowed down and approached her stop. Mary stood up and took her place in the orderly queue that had formed to get off.

It's a pity everybody can't queue up this politely when we're getting on. She thought.

After the stuffy warmth of the bus the damp evening air seemed colder than usual so she fastened the top buttons on her coat and set off to walk the last mile or so to her home. She passed the park and caught the strong scent of blossom in the misty breeze. The smell reminded her of the last holiday they had together. George had scrimped and saved for months without telling her and the first she knew of it was when they were packing their suitcases for two weeks in the Lake District. It was sheer bliss, he made sure of that. What she didn't know was that after the holiday, George was going to give her the bad news about his failing health.

Now she started to recall some of her darker memories - memories which she knew would have been best left hidden in the mists of time. But try as she might, she couldn't blot them out. She seemed to live so much in the past now that once something triggered off a memory it was impossible to stop the pictures flooding into her mind.

As she entered her gate, she mentally chastised herself for once more visiting the more unpleasant memories of her past, vowing never to do so again.

She turned her key in the lock and pushed hard as the front door fought against the day's mail delivery.
"It's me George, I'm home," she shouted.
She picked up the bundle of brown envelopes that tried to bar her entry.
"More bills," she sighed. "It's lucky I've got this job."
She walked into the living room and caught sight of herself in the mirror that hung over the fireplace and went over for a closer look. She looked worn out and more than a little frayed around the edges.
I hope I haven't bitten off more than I can chew, she thought.
After standing for a while silently watching the tears roll down her cheeks, she picked up an urn from the mantelpiece and kissed it.
"George darling," she said aloud. "I love you so much."

THE INHERITANCE

"Don't you think we're a bit old for this?"
"No, if I thought that we wouldn't be here would we? Haven't you heard? 50 is the new 40."
"No need to be so grouchy. What's the matter with you?"
"Nothing! Just shut up and get on with it."
"Very nice! Do you talk to your pupils like that?"
"They don't wind me up like you do."
"Don't you mean *as I do*?"
"What?"
"Well, you're supposed to be an English teacher and you said *like you do* instead of *as you do*."
"Will you shut up you stupid bitch."
"My, my, something's bothering you. We have got a little paddy on today, haven't we?"
His anger causes him to increase his pace and she starts falling behind.
"Hang on, wait for me."
He ignores her and she jogs to catch up and keep pace with him.
"Why did you bring that walking stick?" she gasps.
"It may have escaped your notice, but we are climbing a mountain."
"A mountain? Don't make me laugh. This is Snowdon. You can walk up Snowdon."
"It's still a mountain. Don't underestimate it."
"What's the matter with you lately? Are you worried

about something?"

"Just keep up and stop bothering me."

They plod on and follow the twisting path in silence. Before too long they enter a damp mist which chills them and reduces their vision.

"I think it's time to turn back, don't you?"

"Nonsense!" he replies, "why would we want to do that when we've come this far?"

"Well, it's getting a bit damp for one thing, and didn't that sign say if we're faced with bad weather conditions we should turn back?"

"Rubbish! There's nothing wrong with the weather."

She stays close to him as the thickening mist dampens all sound other than the regular clicking of his walking stick on the rocky pathway.

"You haven't forgiven me have you?"

"Forgiven you for what my dear?"

"For the fact that your uncle Jess left me the house and all his money."

He carries on in silence

"Well?" she persists.

"I don't want to talk about it."

"You'll have to talk about it sometime."

"Oh I will! Don't you worry your grasping little head about *that*."

"There you go again. It wasn't my fault he left it all to me. I was as surprised as you!"

"He was *my* uncle."

"I know he was. Perhaps if you'd spent more time with him ..."

"Like you did you mean? Sorry, *as you did.*"
The mist is now very thick, severely reducing visibility and they slow their pace drastically. She links her arm into his.
"You were sleeping with him, weren't you?"
Her silence tells him all he needs to know. He pulls his arm free from hers and steps back in disgust.
"You asked me a little while ago why I brought this walking stick."
He gives a twist on the cane handle and pulls the shaft away revealing a long steel blade which he plunges through her ribcage and into her heart.
"It was one of uncle Jess's favourite pieces, but of course it belongs to you now. I do hope you enjoy it my dear."

UNWELCOME REUNION

Tommy stood on the narrow ledge with his bare back pressed against the rough brick wall. He carefully tilted his head and looked down. He was three floors up, naked, and terrified.

This is getting a bit much, he thought, *it's time I met someone my own age and settled down.*

Although he was undeniably fit and healthy, at fifty-two, he was getting far too old for this type of behaviour.

He strained to hear the heated argument emanating from the partially open window, which had just served as his escape route.

"I won't ask you again," the man's voice roared. "Whose are they?"

"They're yours," she replied, "they're your old ones. I was having a clear out and found them at the back of the wardrobe. I was going to take them to the charity shop."

"Mine? These are tiny. They would have been too small for me when I was ten years old. You must think I'm a right dickhead. Who is he?"

Tommy shivered on the ledge.

Jesus, he gulped, *the man must be a bloody giant.*

It occurred to him how lucky Jack was to have a beanstalk to climb down.

This was the third time Tommy had been surprised by a husband coming home unexpectedly.

On each of the two previous occasions, the bedrooms had been on the first floor making his escape an easy matter, a small drop from the window ledge, and an embarrassing half-naked streak through the back alleyways.

The sound of furniture being thrown and smashed and the crashing of broken glass made him question why he had always been attracted to other men's wives and girlfriends. Even the guilt he felt when his wife, Mary, died twenty years earlier, failed to stop him. He had constantly cheated on her throughout their twelve years of marriage - starting with one of the bridesmaids who just happened to be engaged to his best friend.

The woman's screams filtered through the window.

"No, No, there's no one out there."

Tommy watched as the window burst fully open and a huge, heavily ridged, Neanderthal head emerged. The bulging eyes almost popped when Tommy came into focus. A meaty hand covered in thick curly hair reached out and tried to grab him by the wrist.

Tommy shuffled along the narrow ledge like a penguin doing an impersonation of a crab.

The head grunted and disappeared back inside, only to reappear seconds later. This time the meaty hand was holding a curtain pole. This time the penguin could not impersonate the crab fast enough and the curtain pole sent Tommy hurtling through the air. He didn't feel a thing.

"Hi, are you Saint Peter?" Tommy asked.

"Do you know what? I'm sick of people asking me that! The first thing everyone says is, 'Are you Saint Peter?' A bit monotonous don't you think? Anyway, never mind who I am, your wife's waiting for you over there."

"My wife?" said Tommy, taken aback.

Tommy looked around and saw Mary walking towards him. She died when she was thirty-two years old and strikingly beautiful. She had not changed a bit.

Tommy drooled as she approached him.

With her full figure, her long blond hair and deep blue eyes, she looked every inch the fashion model she had been when they met.

"Hello Mary," he stammered.

She shook her head from side to side.

"How could you?" she said.

"What? How could I what?"

"All those women! Wasn't I enough for you?"

He bowed his head. "I can't help it; I just can't resist beautiful women."

He tried to put his arms around her but she pushed him away.

"No you don't, I've been chosen to fetch you that's all. Just because we're married doesn't mean you can take advantage of me again."

"Are we still married?"

"Of course we are. The vows last forever."

He smiled. "What happens now?"

"I take you to our new home and we carry on where

we left off before we died. Now give me your hand."
Tommy placed his hand in hers and in an instant they were transported to their home. It was everything Tommy had ever dreamed of. Mary cooked him his favourite curry and gave him a glass of chilled lager to wash it down. After that, they sat on the sofa and watched a film.
"Had I known it was like this when you die I'd have done myself in long ago," he said.
Mary smiled at him and he put his arm around her. She did not object.
"How come you didn't have any curry?"
"I don't eat. We're on a different plane of existence now don't forget. Eating and drinking are optional. I find it a bit messy myself."
"Am I forgiven?" he asked.
"Oh I suppose so," she said, then smiled again and kissed him on the cheek.
"What time's bedtime?" he asked, trying to play it down.
"Whenever you like," she replied, "I usually go up when it goes dark."
He sat counting the seconds for what seemed an eternity. Eventually the light started to fade and his excitement mounted.
Mary yawned and stretched. "I think I'll go up," she said.
He turned the television off and followed her up the stairs to their bedroom.
"It's been a long time," she said, "do you mind

turning away while I get undressed?"

He reluctantly obliged. When he heard her getting into bed, he turned off the light and climbed in alongside her.

Moving towards the middle of the bed, he slowly put his arm around her and cupped her breast.

"Get off."

"I thought we were OK now."

"It's not that, it's just that you're wasting your time. I never feel like it these days. In fact I've never felt like it since I died."

"Erm, I'm not one to blow my own trumpet," he boasted, "but I think you've forgotten how good I am. Let me work my magic and I'm sure you'll change your mind in a few minutes. Know what I mean babe?"

Through the darkness, he caught a glimpse of her smiling lips outlined against the whiteness of the pillow.

"Be my guest," she said.

He slid his hand up towards her breasts as she turned towards him. The silky smooth feel of her bra surprised and pleased him. He tweaked her waiting nipples as she writhed to his touch.

Leaning over, he kissed her full on the lips. She took his hand and guided it down to her scanty knickers. The exquisite feel of the lace and the silk blew his mind. Never before had he derived so much pleasure from the mere touch of his wife's underwear. He tried to imagine what colour they were.

They must be scarlet and black, he thought giving way to his favourite fetish, *only scarlet and black could feel like this.*

He stretched the waist elastic and plunged his hand clumsily inside her knickers, eagerly seeking his ultimate goal. She felt his hand moving slowly at first, then speeding up anxiously.

"OK, I give in," he said, "where is it?"

"I don't have one anymore."

"You don't have one anymore?" he asked in frustration, "what do you mean?"

"Well," she said, grinning and savouring the moment, "I don't eat or drink and I don't have kids, so what would I need that for?"

"I've still got mine," he protested, "and it's always … y'know?"

"Well done you," she smirked, "what are you going to do with it?"

"This can't be right," he complained, "I thought you'd get everything you wanted in heaven."

"You probably do", she sneered, switching on the light, "but this isn't heaven. Heaven is where the real Mary is."

Tommy watched in terror as a pair of ebony-black horns started to grow from her forehead.

THE HOUSE

It was a big squarish framed house that had once been white, but to look at it you could never tell. It was overgrown with moss, and it gave off a green cast through the murky water as I shone my diving torch directly onto the crumbling brick.
I checked the pressure in my tanks. I had plenty of air so I decided to go in.
    The people in the nearby village of Coddleton, had advised me against it. I couldn't find *one* who thought it was a good idea. I could sense their unease as I quizzed them about the history of the place. The pervasive fear and superstition when I broached the subject made it difficult to believe that I was still in twenty-first century Britain. I put this down to the fact that Coddleton was somewhat isolated by the surrounding hills and there was no rail link. The only way in and out was via a badly maintained cinder track, just wide enough for one vehicle at a time, although there were some wider passing points at regular intervals.
In desperation, I resorted to searching the archives of the local newspaper, the Coddleton Gazette, and discovered that the house was the only building in the valley, so when it was decided that the valley should be flooded to create a reservoir to supply the new town of Collinge some twenty miles south, there was little opposition.

While I was trawling through some old copies of the newspaper, something else caught my eye. It was a small report tucked away on page five of the edition for 26th June 2006. Apparently, a man, Terrence Holdsworth, left the comfort of his bed in the early hours of the morning wearing only his pyjamas and babbling incoherently, he made his way to the newly created reservoir, plunged in, and swam until he disappeared from view. His startled wife had been running alongside him, slapping him and trying to wake him, but according to the report, he just kept going as though in a deep trance.
At the inquest she told the coroner that he kept repeating over and over again that, '*the house must 'have its due.*'
Although his body was never found, the inquest concluded that Terrence Holdsworth had drowned in the reservoir.
The thing that shocked and intrigued me most though, was the small headline above the article:
'KILLER HOUSE CLAIMS ITS REVENGE.'
It was then I decided to hire some underwater breathing apparatus and find out more.
I swam around the house until I found the front door, located the handle, and turned it. It wasn't locked, but then why should it be. Who would attempt to burgle an empty house at the bottom of a lake? I pushed it open and shone my torch into the wide
hall, the billowing clouds of silt stirred up by the opening of the door partially obscured my view as I

swam into the murky hallway. I suddenly became aware of some strange feelings and an overwhelming fear stirring within myself.

I thought back to my conversation with the reporter from the Coddleton Gazette and his explanation for the 'KILLER HOUSE' headline. He told me that the people of the village had always regarded the house as haunted in some way. It seemed that anyone visiting it was cursed. Some even died for no apparent reason, while others just seemed to disappear without trace.

He also told me how Terrence Holdsworth had been charged with the duty of checking out the house before the flooding to make sure that nobody was squatting or using it for shelter.

Terrence had claimed the place was empty, but he told his wife some time later that he had been too afraid to approach the house and had falsified his documents.

According to the villagers, as the water rose above the roof of the house, the valley echoed with the sound of banshee-like screeching into the early hours. It was shortly after this that Terrence went missing during his fateful swim, hence the strange newspaper headline about the house exacting revenge.

My fear mounted as I swam the length of the hall and turned left into the reception room and right across to the cellar door. It was all becoming clear now.

I swam down into the cellar and shone my torch in

all directions, hoping with all my being that I wouldn't find anything out of the ordinary. It was then I caught sight of what appeared to be a bundle of rags or some rubbish slowly flapping about in the turbulence my presence had created.

I swam closer for a better view. I wished I hadn't. I was staring at the decomposed remains of Terrence Holdsworth, still wearing his, now rotted, pyjamas.

Worse though, and much more terrifying, was when the ungodly creature that had its arms clasped about his rotting corpse turned to face me.

TWINS

Susan didn't know what to do. It had all started as a silly prank which seemed so funny when she and her twin sister, Jacqueline, had first thought of it. But now, in the cold light of day without the cosy glow of alcohol, she was prey to her ever growing fear.

As the last of the evening light faded, she sat looking at her troubled reflection in the dressing table mirror. There was nothing remotely amusing about the situation now. The humour had long since gone and she wondered how she was going to get out of her promise to Jacqueline. She decided to give it one last try and called out to her sister in the adjoining bedroom.

"Jackie," she sang, "would you come in here a minute please?"

"What now?" Jacqueline rasped, "you're not getting cold feet again are you? You promised."

"I know," replied Susan, "but don't you think it's a bit over the top? I mean what if he notices it's me instead of you? Imagine how embarrassed I'll be ... and him ... both of us."

"Stop worrying," Jacqueline cooed as she tried to cajole her sister, "I've only been out with him three times. There's no way he's going to notice. Mum and Dad still have trouble telling us apart and they've known us nineteen years."

Susan shook her head.

"It's different with boyfriends."

"For goodness sake, he's hardly a boyfriend after three dates," scolded Jacqueline, "You're just using that as an excuse to break your promise. Do what you like, I don't care anymore."

With that she spun hard on her heels and marched out of the room. It was game, set and match. Susan now knew there was no turning back; she *had* to go through with it.

Susan was shivering as she checked her watch yet again. She didn't know if it was because of the cold weather, or the fear of meeting Dave for a date. What she did know was that she would have to be careful. She was worried that she had already made one mistake by turning up early. Jacqueline would never do that, she was always late. She caught sight of her reflection in the window of *Jim's Wine Bar* and saw that her long blonde hair once again had a mind of its own as it swirled about in the gusty breeze.

"No need to worry about whether he'll find me attractive or not," she thought, "if he likes Jackie's looks then he's bound to like mine."

Her thoughts were interrupted as a hackney cab squealed to a halt alongside the kerb and Dave leapt out to join her.

"Hi Jacqueline, sorry I'm late, I had trouble getting a cab."

"Don't worry Dave, you're not late, I'm earl..." She stopped herself short and changed the subject. "You look smart tonight," she went on.

"Thank you," he replied, "but if I look half as smart as you look beautiful, then I'm well pleased."

Susan felt her cheeks flush as she self consciously brushed her hair with her hands. She was pleasantly surprised. From what Jacqueline had told her about Dave, she hadn't expected such a greeting.

She wondered why this same young man had treated her sister to such a display of indifference and bad manners on their nights out."

She looked up into his face. He smiled flashing his perfect white teeth and she realised for the first time just how good looking he was.

Jackie must be mad, she thought, *he's gorgeous.*

"Where shall we go then?" he asked.

"How about *Jim's Wine Bar*, as we arranged," replied Susan pointing behind her. "That is why we arranged to meet here after all."

"Oh, err, yes of course. Sorry, it slipped my mind," Dave said anxiously.

As they entered the wine bar Susan smiled as she felt herself starting to relax. She had been so well briefed by her sister that she could remember things Dave couldn't. Tonight, she decided, she was going to enjoy herself.

When she heard the taxi cab door slam Jacqueline looked out of her bedroom window. It was Susan, as she expected, but there was no sign of Dave. She rushed down the stairs to open the front door, eager to extract the night's news and to share an hour or two laughing and joking at Dave's expense with her sister.

When she opened the door her heart sank.

Susan was sobbing loudly and her face was streaked with a mixture of mascara and tears. It was obvious that she was extremely upset and had been crying for some time. Jacqueline's eyes welled up.

She pulled Susan inside and closed the door. Hugging her tightly, she pushed Susan's head gently against her shoulder and stroked her hair.

"See, I told you he was a rat. What did he do to you?"

Susan tried to pull herself together and spoke through her sobs.

"He didn't do anything to *me*, but he packed *you* in."

"Is that all?" said Jacqueline, "then why all the fuss? Why are you so upset?"

"I don't know," Susan wailed as she broke free from her sister's arms and ran crying up the stairs to her bedroom.

The next day Susan had calmed down enough to tell her sister about the events of the previous evening. Jacqueline was surprised to hear what a perfect gentleman Dave had been, and how well Susan had got on with him.

"I don't understand it," she said, "how come he was so nice? How could he have changed so much?"

"He must have decided at the start of the evening that he was going to pack me...I mean you, in, so he probably decided that he'd make an effort for the last date," guessed Susan.

"Well all I can say is that it's a pity he didn't behave like that earlier. If he had, I might have made more of an effort myself. Ah well, plenty more fish in the sea."

Susan didn't say so, but she wished she could hook this particular fish for herself. She was feeling hurt and rejected. She had always scorned the idea of love at first sight, yet the feelings she had were so strong she wondered if she'd ever get over him.

Some weeks later, Susan was at the local shopping centre when a familiar voice stopped her dead in her tracks.

"Hello Jacqueline, how are you?"

"Oh, hello Dave," she replied, "I'm not Jacqueline, I'm Susan, her twin sister."

"That's a relief," he laughed, "because I'm not Dave, I'm Steven, *his* twin brother."

"What do you mean?" she asked, "if this is some sort of joke you'll have to tell me the punch line because I don't get it."

"You're very like your sister aren't you? Come on, I'll buy you a coffee and tell you all about it."

Susan listened agog as Steven told her that he and Dave were identical twins, and how much Dave resented the fact.

"It embarrasses him no end," laughed Steven, "I think it's because of the way Mum used to dress us the same when we were kids. Everybody in the family fussed over us like mad and I don't think he ever got over it. I bet he didn't even tell your Jacqueline he was a twin."

"No he didn't. She didn't have a clue."

Susan furrowed her brow in puzzlement.

"Hang on a minute, if you've never met our Jackie, then how do you know I'm like her?"

The silence that followed was unbearable as Steven got more flustered by the second. Then he decided he could stand it no longer.

"OK, I'll tell you, but first of all you've got to promise me that you'll never tell your Jacqueline."

"Go on," she prompted.

"Give me your word first," he insisted.

Susan paused for a second and mentally balanced her loyalty to Jacqueline against her own curiosity...it was no contest.

"OK, you have my word," she said.

Steven then told Susan about how he and Dave had rowed because Dave was going to stand Jacqueline up on their last date, and how Dave had suggested sarcastically that if he was so worried about it, then he should go in his place.

"How come he changed his mind?" she asked.

"He didn't. I went instead," replied Steven, "the sad part is, we got on great together and by the end of the night I'd fallen for her, but because of our Dave I had to tell her that I didn't want to see her again. I wanted to tell her the truth and ask her out myself, but she was hardly in the mood. How is she now anyway?"

"Oh she's fine," Susan smiled, "she's not bothered."

Steven smiled back at her. "Are *you* doing anything on Saturday night?"

"Well, I've nothing planned, but I wouldn't mind another date with you."

"Another date with me?" he asked. "What do you mean?"

"I mean it was me you met on that last date. Our Jacqueline was going to stand your Dave up. I didn't think it was right so I went in her place."

They smiled broadly and locked into each other's gaze.

A FACE IN THE CROWD

He looked across the crowded lawn and caught her looking anxiously at him. It made him feel most uncomfortable. Limping out of her line of sight and into the marquee, he ignored the crowd and barged his way over to the line of trestle tables that occupied the far side of the tent.

He picked up a polystyrene cup and sipped at the tea it contained. It was so weak it tasted almost like hot water. He looked at the large array of food trays before him. Confused by such a large choice, he picked up a few different sandwiches and sniffed them closely before returning them to the tray. He finally settled on a salmon sandwich and although it felt a bit damp and doughy, he bit into it. *How can something that smells so foul taste so good*, he thought. He sniffed the sandwich with every bite as though addicted to the strong fishy smell. When he finished, he wiped his hands on the front of his trousers and wandered out of the marquee again.

He inhaled the scent of the freshly mown grass. It smelled ever sweeter when contrasted with the unpleasant, yet intriguing, smell of the soggy salmon sandwich. Squinting as the bright July sunlight hurt his eyes, he found an unoccupied bench and eased himself down into a sitting position, facing away from the offending sun, now he felt its searing heat on the back of his neck.

He became aware of his heavy breathing. The short walk had left him gasping for air. He reached for his tea but it wasn't there. He was forgetting things all the time now and guessed he must have left it somewhere, remembering where though, was another matter. Scanning the lawn once again he noticed the advanced age of most of the crowd and could sense the uneasy atmosphere. He did not want to be here but there was no other choice.

Not many youngsters here, he thought. It was then he saw her looking at him again. This time she was talking to two of the younger uniformed women. He was sure they were talking about him. His suspicions were confirmed when she started pointing at him and saying something. Both the uniformed women looked at him and started nodding at the her in agreement.

His feelings of discomfort returned. He struggled to his feet and made his slow, but steady, way around the back of the red brick building and out of sight of the bustling lawn.

He knew if he stayed in one place too long she'd find him again and that would just make things even more difficult. He couldn't handle the tears every time she caught up with him. She used to be the most important person in his life, but he wondered about that now. This place had destroyed their relationship, perhaps it was beyond repair. Maybe she was glad to be rid of him.

All he wanted was to be back home with her, sitting

on the sofa watching television and drinking lots of tea. His head started aching again, it was even hurting him to think clearly these days.

He wondered how much she'd really miss him. One thing was for sure, his life was never going to be the same again. He wondered if she'd be able to cope on her own.

Tears flowed as he tried to convince himself she was going to be alright.

"God forgive me," he said aloud, "but I couldn't look after her any more, I'm too old."

He took his car keys from his pocket, opened the door and struggled to get in. Sitting in the driver's seat, he looked across at the empty passenger seat and remembered her crying like a child as he eased her out of the car. It reminded him of the way their daughter had cried on her first day at school. He looked up again at the foreboding walls of the secure care home and thought about how his own memory was rapidly fading. He knew it wouldn't be long before he was forced to join her here. In the latter stages of their lives they would probably pass each other in the sterile, highly polished corridors without recognition.

He wondered why older people clung on so tightly to the small amount of worthless life they had left and collapsed in a flood of tears.

CYCLE

He watched the monitor with increasing sadness as the blue planet he now knew as Earth grew ever smaller on the screen. Soon it would be indistinguishable from the other billions of stars and planets that formed the galaxy the astronomers of his home planet had catalogued as X581963, although he would now always remember it as *The Milky Way*.
Turning away from the screen, he realised that his life would never be the same again, he would always have fond memories of the new friends he had made on Earth. He missed them more than he had ever thought possible.
This was the first time he had ever come into contact with mammalian life. All the beings on his own planet were reptilian. He had read of the evolution of early mammalian life forms in his planet's early history. Unfortunately, they proved to be a source of highly nutritious food for his ancestors who hunted them to extinction. The Earth-dwellers had fascinated him. He wondered at their closeness and how they genuinely cared for each other. How they sacrificed their own happiness for the benefit of others and how their close knit families and communities coexisted. They spoke a great deal of love and he wondered what it must be like to experience such a powerful emotion.
Thinking back to his own upbringing, he couldn't

help but feel envious of the human mammals.

He remembered how he fought his way through the thick shell of the egg he was formed in. The adults showed no compassion as they counted the newly hatched arrivals. Any that lost the immense struggle to emerge to a new life were discarded without a care. No tears ever ran down the scales of a reptile face. Social co-operation was merely a tool to help the race progress which, in turn, led to many individual benefits. He couldn't understand how he had managed to bridge the gap and empathise with the humans. It seemed that his short stay on their planet had allowed him to overcome millions of years of his own evolution.

Perhaps, he thought, *these feeling have always been with me and they just needed kindling.*

Whatever the reason, he had made good friends with some of them and even though he would eventually be billions of light years from them, they would always have a place in his heart.

He tried to switch off his thoughts deeming them to be non-productive because he knew he would never see these, or any other human beings again, but there was also something else niggling away in his brain, something he could not quite put his finger on.

what is it? he thought.

He was interrupted as the captain's voice boomed over the star ship's intercom.

"Will all non-essential crew members who have requested induced hibernation please attend the medical bay within the next twelve hours."

He thought about the captain's announcement. Intergalactic travel was always boring, and he imagined that this trip would seem particularly so. Not only because of his emotional state, but also because of the constant niggle that seemed to be eating away at his brain ... if only he could fathom it out.

Perhaps he, himself should make a late application for hibernation. This would free him from the strange, sentimental feelings he had been having lately - at least for the duration of the trip. When life was back to normal on his home planet all these feelings would fade and just become a distant memory.

He remembered the time he was ravaged by the three-legged Snuggle Sisters from Alpha 5. At the time, he had not been emotionally mature enough to cope with their voracious sexual appetites and their strange ways. The memories of this encounter had been so traumatic that he was unable to sleep properly for months, but now they didn't seem to bother him so much.

Time is a great healer he thought, *and what better way to pass time than in a state of hibernation.*

After he sought permission from the captain, the medical team agreed to his request for hibernation and he was put to sleep. He became totally oblivious of the long homeward journey.

He was awakened by a series of mild slaps on his

face.

"We are about to enter our solar system," advised the voice of one of the medical staff.

Opening his eyes, he grinned broadly.

"I know what it is," he said aloud, "I know what it is that's been niggling away at me all this time. I must see the captain urgently."

He jumped off the resuscitation bunk and made his way through the labyrinthine corridors that led to the captain's quarters. Knocking on the door, he rushed in without waiting to be invited. The captain looked up from his desk surprised.

"Hello ET," he said, "what can I do for you?"

"We need to turn around and go back to Earth captain," ET gasped breathlessly, "I've forgotten my bicycle."

THE PARTY

Simon smiled warmly as he watched Leanne putting the final touches to her make-up in front of the dressing table mirror.

'She's absolutely gorgeous,' he thought, *'it's no wonder I love her so much.'*

He thought back to the night they first met in the Caradoc Hotel near the Dock Road in Bootle. There was no doubt it was love at first sight for both of them. Within two weeks of meeting they set up home together. That was nine months ago and there was no sign of their passion cooling. If anything, they were even more in love and couldn't bear to be apart.

Early on in their relationship, Simon wondered if the joy and elation he felt when he and Leanne were together was because he was 'on the rebound' from his recent split with Mary, his fiancée of seven years. He wondered if the split distorted his feelings and he wasn't really in love with Leanne at all, but as the days went by and their new relationship grew stronger, Mary faded into a ghostly memory. A kind of faded brown, detached memory like the picture of his lost-at-sea Granddad that Nan used to have on her mantelpiece.

Simon knew the party was being thrown by mutual friends of his and Mary's. He also knew she had been invited and was going to be there.

'Boy is she in for a surprise,' he mused, *'wait 'til she sees*

how gorgeous Leanne is.'

Mary grinned as she put her hand inside John's denim jacket and tweaked his nipple.

"Not while I'm driving if you don't mind," laughed John, "there'll be plenty of time for that sort of thing later!"

Mary's grin changed to a warm smile as she admired John's manly profile.

'This is the man I've been waiting for all my life,' she thought, *'all those wasted years with that no-hoper, Simon. Thank God I broke it off when I did. We'd have drifted into old age still engaged and drawing our pension.'*

Her thoughts were interrupted by John's smooth baritone voice.

"I hate to be a nuisance, but aren't you supposed to be giving me directions?"

"Sorry John, I was miles away. Take the next left and second on the right and we're there. Number thirty-three Lonsdale Mews."

John pinched his nostrils together to distort his voice. "Wilco leader, over and out."

Mary laughed loudly at John's Biggles impersonation and playfully punched him on his arm. His bizarre sense of humour was one of the things she loved most about him. That and his caring sensitivity. The fact that he was a dead ringer for George Clooney was an added bonus. Mary knew that Simon was going to be at the party. She couldn't wait to see his face as she introduced him to John.

Simon paid the cab driver, linked arms with Leanne and walked up the path of number thirty-three Lonsdale Mews. The door was open so they walked straight in to the sound of loud, welcoming voices.
Their hosts greeted them and gave each a large glass of wine. Simon scanned the crowd carefully,
hoping to catch sight of Mary.
"Late as usual," he murmured under his breath.

John finally managed to find a parking space and became aware of Mary's growing impatience.
"Slow down Mary," he said, "it's only ten to eight.
I think they just might have some booze left if we're lucky."
Mary pulled at his arm as he used his remote control to lock the car.
"I don't want to be late," she said.
They entered the house and received the same warm welcome and hospitality as Simon and Leanne moments earlier. Mary slowly looked about her. She looked through the kitchen door and caught sight of Simon talking to a tall, good looking blonde girl.
'He's got no chance with her,' she thought bitterly, *'she's beautiful! Far too good looking to fall for him.'*
As the night wore on, Mary saw Simon standing alone.
'Yes!' she thought, *'here's my chance.'*
She pulled John's arm and headed over to Simon.

"There's someone I'd like to meet."
She guided him through the crowded lounge and out into the kitchen.
"Hi Simon, this is John," she gloated.
Simon smiled weakly at John and dutifully shook his hand. Seconds later, Leanne returned and stood alongside Simon, who now put his smile on full beam. He introduced Leanne to both John and Mary. Introductions over, both Mary and Simon feigned indifference and continued to circulate.
The music got louder, the dancing got more hectic, and the drink flowed faster.
When everyone had their fill and it was time to go, the inevitable queue of guests waiting to retrieve their coats from the bedroom formed like a Hokey Cokey snake all the way up the stairs.
That's when it happened.
A disagreement about ownership of a particular coat gave way to some pushing and shoving. One of the guests went flying through a bedroom door furthur along the landing.
The hush that followed was palpable. In the spotlight cast by the open door, lay two startled, perspiring, naked people in flagrante delicto ... Leanne and John.

WHAT HAPPENED IN THE PLAYGROUND

I can't believe it. How could I have been so stupid? The doctors have sectioned me for forty-eight hours and they're saying they might need to extend it for twenty-eight days if I don't get back to normal soon. They said they had to section me to give me the medication needed to calm me down. I'm being kept under close observation at the moment to see if I recover OK.

Mum and dad came in to the hospital to see me. They were furious. I made them even worse by laughing at their sad faces. I wouldn't normally do this, but I was still on a high from the stuff I'd taken. Dad gave me the old lecture about how disappointed he was and how I was letting everyone down, especially myself.

It was mum I felt sorry for though. She was crying her eyes out. She said we'd never had anyone mad in our family before.

Even the police didn't know how to deal with me. In the end they called an ambulance and came with me to hospital. They held me down while the doctor gave me an injection. Thank God they did, I don't know what I might have ended up doing. I was like a wild animal by then. I even tried to bite one of the coppers.

It all started when I read on the net about the new drugs that people were inventing, not top scientists, just ordinary people like me who could find their

way around the chemistry lab.
According to the blog they could give you a real buzz with none of the side effects that E's and smack had. The beauty of it is, these drugs are so new, that there are no laws to cover them and you can't get done. By the time they've made them illegal you just change the chemical structure a bit and it's legal again. There's a lot of money to be made and I decided I was going to get my hands on some of it.
I started getting into school an hour early every day and sneaking into the lab. With all the information available on the internet and my own basic knowledge of chemistry it didn't take long for me to start getting some results.
The first ones only gave a slight buzz that didn't last long and some of them even made me feel sick, but after a while, as I began to get better at using the equipment, they were getting so good I was lifted for the whole day.
The one I made last Monday made me feel so alive that I decided it was time to test the market and sell some of it.
That night, Mum and Dad sat downstairs watching Coronation Street, blissfully unaware that I'd turned my bedroom into a drugs den. I carefully measured the doses out and wrapped them in silver foil. Curiosity got the better of me so I took one myself and set off giggling all the way to the local youth club. I sold thirty three deals for a tenner each in less than two hours - three hundred and thirty quid - not

a bad night's work. Before long though some of my customers started going off their heads attracting too much attention. I had to get off sharpish.

This morning, I tried a new formula off the net. It was a new posting and the person who put it on said to be careful, but I of course knew better. I was in a hurry and didn't want to be late for class, so I don't know whether I mixed it wrong or what, but my head exploded as soon as I took it. Everything went hazy and the next thing I remembered was being out in the schoolyard at break.

We've got a real good looking, young teaching assistant in our school. Her name is Chantelle and I've always had the impression she fancied me. Normally I'm dead shy when it comes to talking to girls, but this morning, because I was off my head with the drugs, I felt so full of confidence that I was chatting Chantelle up as though we'd known each other for years. We went behind the Bike sheds and started kissing each other. She was loving it. Who'd have thought a gorgeous woman like her would fancy me? Anyway, the noise of the kids egging us on attracted the attention of the headmistress, old Maggie Henshaw. Me and Chantelle were well at it by the time she'd battled her way through the crowd and appeared at the back of the sheds. She nearly had a fit and started raging at us.

'Piss off you dried up old hag,' I shouted, 'can't you see we're enjoying ourselves?'

She stormed off in disgust, the kids all cheering that

someone had finally stood up to her.

I don't know how long it was exactly because I'd lost track of time with the drugs, but soon I was being pulled across the playground by two big coppers and I took a nasty turn. I broke free and started smashing the school windows with anything I could lay my hands on, bricks, sports equipment, lunch boxes, I even snatched a guitar off one of the first year kids and wellied it, pointy end first, right through the big reception hall window.

Eventually, the coppers caught me again, and this time they weren't gonna let me go. They sat on me until the ambulance came and you know the rest.

Just after mum and dad left, the headmistress, Old Maggie Henshaw, called in to see if I was OK. She said that I had done enormous damage to the school's reputation. The local press had turned up taking photos, and some of the kids had videoed the whole thing and put it on YouTube. Mrs Henshaw said it had gone viral; especially the part with me and Chantelle snogging. She said she didn't think I'd ever be allowed back into the school, but if I was, I'd definitely have to relinquish my position as Deputy Headmaster.

THE PRISONER'S TALE

I'm a very jealous person. What's mine is mine, and what's mine stays mine. I'm not particularly proud of it, that's just the way I am. I've always been like that for as long as I can remember. When I was a kid, I was the type who stamped on any sweets I dropped just to stop anybody else from picking them up and eating them. If any of my classmates got a new game or toy I was green with envy. Not a good way to live I know, but you are what you are. Don't get me wrong, I've tried to change many times, but just like the good old leopard, *I* can't change my spots either. I remember when I was twelve and my best mate got a brand new bike for his birthday. I felt so bad that I avoided him and didn't speak to him for days. This was followed by delight when I heard through the grapevine that it had been stolen three days later.

As I consoled him, wearing the saddest expression I could muster, my delight turned into sheer bliss when he told me that the bike wasn't insured.

Thus was the pattern of my life as I choreographed my way with facial expressions and actions to suit every purpose. Few ever guessed my real feelings.

My problem worsened when I started dating girls. If there was a pretty girl around I couldn't stand the idea that others boys were looking at her. I realised that I couldn't have every girl on the planet but my inner feelings were beyond logical rationalisation.

I eventually started going out with a girl who was absolutely gorgeous. She had the looks of a film star or a model, not only that, but she was also a lovely warm and caring person. I was besotted with her. One Saturday night we were at a dance. I hated the idea, but she loved dancing so I agreed to go. Before long she was asked to dance by a tall, slim good looking feller. They were dancing really well and looked great together as I stood at the bar, seething, and counting the seconds to the end of the song. I was just about holding it together when it happened. I saw his hand slide from the small of her back down to her bum. The next thing I knew was that he was lying on the floor groaning and one of the bar stools had become part of his gums.

Six months free accommodation in Walton Prison was my reward for that creative episode. It was a nightmare. Everyone's after your gear, chocolate, toothpaste, fags if you've got any, anything at all. If you've got it, someone wants it. One con even wanted to borrow my toothbrush. I wouldn't have minded so much but his halitosis was so bad that the screws had to keep checking his kecks just to make sure. I got into so many scuffles trying to protect my stuff that I lost all my remission and ended up doing the full sentence. When I *was* eventually released I vowed never to go 'inside' again.

I made the usual smooth transition from prison cell to benefits and bedsit land and tried to get on with my life while keeping my head down.

As the years rolled on I kept to myself, in fact it's fair to say that by the time I was thirty, I'd become a bit of a recluse. I wasn't happy with this. I longed for company. I longed to share my life with someone without being jealous – or so I thought. In reality, I didn't know the meaning of the word *share*. In truth it was alien to me. I didn't know it then, but I've since learned that my concept of sharing is ownership and control, and the root emotion underlying my jealousy is an overwhelming desire to control.

Eventually, through sheer desperation, I had an idea. I'd find the ugliest woman I could and marry her. She'd have to be so ugly that nobody else could ever fancy her. I brushed aside intrusive thoughts of mantelpieces and poking fires and set about my plan. First I drew up a list of my requirements. Ugly was a given – the uglier the better, she'd have to have no sense of fashion at all, maybe a bit on the plump side but not fat, no fashionable hair styles, maybe a few hairs on the chin would be good. Age? Forty to forty-five perhaps, quite a bit older than me anyway! She mustn't smell though. I definitely don't want a stinker!

I set off on my quest full of hope and enthusiasm, having decided to try the local bars and singles clubs first. I saw some real ugly women all right, but what annoyed me was that however ugly they were, there was always some man looking at them with an amorous glint in his eye.

I needed someone who nobody else fancied in the

least.

After a few weeks I saw her. I followed her from bar to bar and watched as she ordered her drinks. Not one head turned to look at her. She might as well have been invisible. She looked like a Dalek with a straw wig on, and had a voice to match. Perfect I thought as I went over to introduce myself. I bought her a drink and she gave me a smile that seemed more of a grimace and told me her name was Ethel.

As we all know, beauty is a subjective thing with no real scientific means of measurement. Suffice it to say, that if Helen of Troy's face was so beautiful it was reputed to have launched a thousand ships, then, at a push, Ethel's beauty might have been just enough to launch a kayak on the Leeds to Liverpool canal.

I was overjoyed and we spent the rest of the night getting to know each other. Surprisingly, we got on very well. Ethel had a great sense of humour and there was nothing pretentious about her at all. I was so comfortable in her company. We agreed to see each other the next night, and the next, and the next. Before long we were inseparable. It bothered me somewhat that I had such feelings for her but she was the first person I could truly be myself with, and the truth was, something that I hadn't remotely considered happened. I'd fallen in love with her. When I proposed to her at our favourite restaurant she honked loudly with laughter and told me to go to and see an optician.

Our wedding was a quiet affair followed by a honeymoon at a rented cottage in the Lake District. For the first time in my life I was truly happy. I loved Ethel with all my heart and started to notice other things about her. The warmth she displayed in her crooked smile, the twinkle in her eye as she pulled my leg, how well she could cook. Her aura filled the room when she entered, and the sex? The sex was fabulous. I learned that beauty *really is* in the eye of the beholder.

After the honeymoon I got a job as a landscape gardener and we bought a small cottage together in Ainsdale, near Southport. I took driving lessons and we eventually got a car. All my old psychological problems seemed to melt away and I became a fully functioning, normal person. It seemed I drew strength from Ethel, as she did from me. We lived our lives in a constant haze of bliss.

One day it rained so heavily and constantly that I finished work early. On the way home I bought a bottle of wine and a box of Ethel's favourite chocolates to surprise her, but it was me who got the surprise. When I opened the front door I heard grunting noises coming from our bedroom. I made my way upstairs expecting to find Ethel doing her keep fit exercises. I opened the door and there was Ethel and this strange man, bang at it in our bed.

I felt my head popping as all of my old feelings flooded back into me. I dragged the man backwards by his hair.

Unfortunately for him, he'd left his white stick laying next to the bedside cabinet so I picked it up and laid into him. Not only did I give him *'what for'* but I added a few *'that's why's'* as well.

Three weeks after I beat him up, his family gave their consent to turn off his life support machine as there was no hope of a recovery. They wouldn't allow Ethel to go to his funeral.

She keeps asking me to allow her visiting permits. I'd never say yes though. I'd just be wondering who she's been with. It's not too bad in here this time. Being a lifer, I've got my own room and my own stuff around me. It's a bit like my old bedsit really. They say that with good behaviour I could be out in eight years.

I'm not sure that's what I want though – I don't think I could cope.

TED WATKINS, THE SALT OF THE EARTH

Ted Watkins was born and bred on the poor side of town. Ever since he could remember he had been totally opposed to the way the world's resources were unfairly allocated. He hated the injustice of the way children on the posh side of town were given the best of everything, while he and his friends often went without.

As he grew older, he realised that this was not just a local thing. No, he was in fact quite lucky to be born where there was any food at all. He became aware that in certain parts of the world, people died from starvation while a tiny percentage of extremely greedy people controlled most of the world's wealth for themselves alone.

He wanted to do something to redress the balance. *But how can a poor, insignificant guy like me help,* he often thought.

Ted's idea came in a flash of inspiration. On Whit Monday, 26th of May, 2020 he was standing bare footed with his trousers rolled up on Southport beach waiting for the tide to come in. The fact that he had such a large amount of time on his hands started him thinking.

All that water out there, he mused, *If only we could turn that into food, nobody need ever go hungry again.*

That was when he got the idea for his machine.

For the next three months he spent most of his time

in the garden shed inventing and constructing an atomic conversion machine. This machine could convert water into any substance known to man. It worked by deconstructing the atomic structure of the water in the deconstruction chamber, then, through a series of further chambers and specific processes, reconverting the sub-atomic particles into any element, or combination of elements that had been scanned in the analysis chamber..

The wide ranging versatility of the machine was of little interest to Ted. His only interest in developing it was to feed the starving people of the world. The ability to convert water into protein, fat and carbohydrates, meant that everybody in the world would be able to eat to their heart's content. This, and this alone, had been the driving force behind Ted's desire to create his replicating machine.

Financial considerations and public acclaim had played no part whatsoever. No great wealth or knighthood for him. Mankind's *'hand on his shoulder smote,'* would be acknowledgement enough. With the world's food needs met in full, *sodden red sand of deserts* would be consigned to literature and history.

Ted filled in the usual patent application which gave him protection for one year. This allowed interested parties their chance to contest his right to the invention of the machine.

If they could prove that the techniques used by Ted's machine already existed in one form or another, then his patent would be denied. It also gave the Ministry of Defence the right to confiscate any inventions that were deemed to have any military value.

Everybody considered Ted to be a crank - until he went public and gave a live demonstration on News at Ten. He replicated a litre of unleaded petrol in one millisecond. This made the petrol companies open their eyes and prick up their collective ears. They got their sharp suited lawyers to bombard Ted with meaningless writs just to keep him occupied while they formed a real plan. Then they took him to court arguing that a cow's digestion system already does what Ted's machine could do - and has done so for thousands of years.

Although the ensuing court case delayed Ted's production by nine months, the final ruling of the three appeal judges was that:

'the fact nature has imbued cows with the ability to use a series of chambers to convert grass into milk does not constitute prior knowledge of Ted's invention.'

It was such a great relief to him. He had beaten the might of the oil companies.

He hardly had time to draw breath when he received notification that the government, who had been closely following the court case, deemed his invention to hold considerable military potential and would be taking control of it. The fact that he would be well compensated meant nothing to him.

The reason he built the machine was to feed the world, not to make money.

Before the cumbersome and inertia-laden procedure

of the Ministry of Defence could grind into action, he filled a suitcase, packed his machine in a crate and booked a sea passage to China. A country where he hoped people would understand his desire to feed the starving people of the world.

Human beings and rumour mills being what they are, it wasn't too long into the voyage when news of this mysterious machine caught the captain's ear. Being a curious man, the captain insisted on seeing the machine for himself.

As the ship approached the Mariana Islands, Ted was almost where he wanted to be anyway, so he reluctantly agreed to give a demonstration of his invention's powers. He set the machine up on the deck, explaining to the ever growing crowd of crew and passengers as he did so, that the converter used the residual sub-atomic particles to power itself. That was why it didn't need to be plugged in. It was totally independent of any power source. As long as it had a supply of water in the disassembly chamber it would run forever. As the captain arrived, Ted asked the crowd if they had any items he could use to replicate in his machine. An old lady dipped into her plastic shopping bag and handed him a Toastie loaf and a toilet roll. Ted placed them into the analysis chamber, pulled the lever and stood back.

Within seconds the deck was full of toilet rolls and Toastie loaves. Ted battled against the tide of groceries and switched the lever to *off*. Amazed, the captain asked how many of each item was on the deck. Ted guessed that the machine had been running for about two seconds,

"Two thousand," he said, "it replicates once every millisecond, so it's about two thousand."

As he spoke, a huge wave slapped the side of the ship causing her to list almost thirty degrees. Ted's machine slid across the deck and caught its lever on the bottom rope of the ship's rail, switching it on.

As the passengers and crew grabbed on to anything they could, they watched the machine spewing out toilet rolls and loaves of bread as it splashed into the water, destined for the Mariana Trench – the deepest part of the ocean.

Thursday 26th May 2220

Ted Watkins' great, great, great, great, great, great, great, great, great, great grandson, Herbert, clambered and trudged wearily over the matted paper landscape. He'd heard that they were selling fresh water at two thousand pounds per litre in the town centre. At that price he couldn't afford to miss out.

He remembered the stories he'd heard about the rich people bathing in their posh bathrooms then selling off their used bathwater for the poor people to drink.

In his rage he kicked out and burst his foot through the orange, greaseproof wrapping paper of yet another Toastie loaf.

'If only somebody could build a machine to convert all this

bread and paper into water,' he thought. *'If only.'*

Printed in Great Britain
by Amazon